THE TRIAL
TOURNAMENT OF HEARTS
BOOK I

AUSTIN VALENZUELA

V

WHAT EVERYONE CAN'T SEE

R hea had too much anxiety to send such risky texts.

She swiped up on her phone, refreshing her direct messages underneath the teacher's desk when a scream came from the right half of the classroom, followed by a fit of laughter from a group of nagging students.

"That's not funny!" yelled Olivia Ragen, a blond girl who'd spent far too much time play-flirting with a particular third grader in her class. This boy was sweet and tolerated most of her teasing, but it was only a matter of time before the kid grew tired of putting up with her taunts. Apparently, he got his revenge with a few friends and ended up catching Olivia off-guard.

"Mike, Chandler, Tommy!" Rhea shouted. The three troublemakers turned their heads in succession, guilt written across their faces. "Leave Olivia alone." All she had to do was shoot a scornful gaze toward Olivia for her to get the point.

Rhea swiped down on her phone screen again. She'd been peeking all day, trying to maintain a casual conversation with tonight's potential date. Her anxiety spiked at the sight of a little blue dot next to his name. The message's preview jumped out at her before she had time to open it.

How does seven o'clock sound? I think I know a place that—
"Miss Williams?"

Rhea shoved her phone back into her pocket, looking up to see Jonathan Yang, another kind boy who always asked if he could play outside. Tears streamed down his cheeks. He held the second recorder she'd given him since lessons began a few days ago; it was split in half.

By the welling tears in his eyes and stammering bottom lip, she imagined he thought he was in trouble. "I-I-"

"Don't worry, sweetheart." *Find a quick solution*, she told herself, making her way around the desk to crouch in front of the boy as he sniffled and rubbed puffy eyes. "Would you like a better recorder? One that's even more fun to play?" *Easier and less breakable,* she thought under her fostered smile. She didn't know how much more "teaching" she could take.

She didn't hate the kids. At first, she even loved the rascals, thinking an elementary school teacher would be a great gig while she applied to orchestras, schools, and tours; while she tried to be a *real* musician. She didn't know how time-consuming, soul-sucking, and mind-numbing teaching actually was. It wasn't Jonathan Yang's fault that he'd been born with hands more skilled at gripping a baseball bat than swiftly gliding along a flute. She needed to remind herself of this, and the near impossibility of getting young boys to sit quietly for more than a few hours, or her response would've been entirely inconsiderate.

"Honey," she said, "tell me what you want to do to solve this. Wallowing in your tears doesn't do any good."

Jonathan nodded his head vigorously. He was a strong kid.

"Do you want the new flute?" she asked.

He nodded his head again, sniffling a little less.

"I think that's a good idea. Let's go grab it."

They walked amongst howling, loose notes without aim and squeaking cries from plugged instruments toward the back of the room, decorated with paintings from students who liked her for whatever reason. Rhea hardly noticed these sounds because of the phone burning a hole through her jean pocket, into her thigh.

He actually wants to go on a date.

A nervous energy filled her. It'd been months since her last date... *more*. So long she'd stopped counting.

Already, ideas of inviting him home filled her head, along with worries about the cleanliness of her bedroom. She hadn't put up any fall decorations, either.

But did the interior decor even matter when it came to hooking up? How often did men come over and comment on her marble countertops? What was Tinder *really* for?

It would be her first true hook-up through the app. The very thought of her night progressing made her chest tight with anticipation. She told herself it was natural to be nervous, and he certainly couldn't care less about whether she was festive, or the state of her home. Again, if Tinder wasn't about sex, why else would the app ask people to judge others based on nothing but pictures, age, and a short personal bio?

Needless to say, she was desperate.

She kept her supplies on a shelf where students couldn't reach them. Flutes were in a bucket to the far left. She pushed to the bottom and grabbed one of the few Sopranos left, marked by their faded coloring and the number *2016* written on the side in sharpie. The ratio of wood to plastic on these models leaned so far on the side of toy soldier that she could chuck it against the wall and it wouldn't chip.

With the recorder in hand, she bent down again to Jonathan's level. The boy had almost stopped crying. Rhea couldn't believe how similar little kids were to attention-seeking adults.

She thought she felt her phone vibrate in her pocket, but there was no new message.

"Now, this is a very special recorder." She handed it over, pointing at the grooves on the side. "These marks tell you exactly where to hold it. You'll play ten times better if you put your fingers there."

Jonathan's eyes widened.

"Maybe even twenty. It's the truth," she said, encouraging him to go play with the other kids who already watched in stillness, envying his special meeting with the teacher.

That should buy me some time.

Rhea leaned against the back wall of the classroom, surveying the space to make sure everyone was being nice to Jonathan, who they just saw cry. Rhea felt it wasn't entirely wrong to reward the boy for showing his emotions, though she did see the fault in giving him a new recorder every time he broke his old one.

But what did she know about teaching children? *What does anyone know? There are just a bunch of conflicting theories.* Rhea wasn't even thirty. If she were to have a kid, people would say she was a child herself. Maybe that was why she found herself googling a thousand different ways to get kids to listen.

She shifted her balance in an effort to discreetly check her new message. Its author went by the username, *Llswole*, otherwise known as Laird Lorenson. According to his Instagram and Tinder profiles, he could have one of two personalities. The first personality was a douchey body-builder who posed in front of the gym mirror for muscle pictures, as indicated from the nearly six-hundred Instagram photos with his shirt pulled halfway up his body, displaying a six-pack that would've been impressive if it weren't beneath such a smug grin. She was fit but not gym-rat fit, something like young Mariah Carey meets Kim K, when people were being nice (or trying to get in her tight-fitting jeans), and over time the pasta and sweets she ate would probably throw off his rice and chicken regimen. The second personality, discernable through his Tinder profile, told of a sweet, honest soul who enjoyed spending time with his family and occasionally the "bros"— who were considerably more attractive, if she was being honest.

Both personalities shone through in his texting style. Was it possible that he was a deep man, capable of a broad range of human emotion? Of course. But she had also dated gym rats before, and it was equally, if not more possible that he was a narcissistic sociopath using Tinder to manipulate women and get some action. It was one of those situations that she would have to feel out on the first date.

How does seven o'clock sound? I think I know a place that serves great Ramen noodles. I can only eat their rice bowls, but you can get whatever you like. Especially if you're my girl.

Rhea shoved her phone back into her pocket. There it was. A cute, gentleman-like proposition to take her to dinner, followed by flirting so clumsy that it practically slapped her across the face. She crossed her arms and looked out into the sea of kids. "Remember to play with inside volume."

Whoever Laird was, if he had the balls to call her his girl when they hadn't even met in person, there was no telling what he'd have the balls to do on a first date. She'd be open to going home with some guy... if he wasn't visibly nuts.

And yes, she knew there were better men out there, better jobs and a bigger world. She knew she had the mind to be something great. But the logistics of it all fucked everything up. This world wasn't the work-hard-and-get-everything-you-want place she'd been promised. Rhea could hardly afford drinks with her friends, let alone move away to start a new life in an area with hundreds of eligible bachelors. Her shitty scenario seemed to double as a coffin.

This is it. These kids and this shitty school. These terrible dating options. This was the life she'd been destined to live. Thinking of her parents, they also seemed to realize that they needed to settle for average, because that was all there would ever be. Her father had given up his dream of doing animation for Disney, while her mother found a passion in living the most ordinary life she possibly could. If Rhea had to spend the rest of her life looking forward to bingo at the neighborhood Greenwise, she would rather be poor and estranged. But she also didn't dare to go broke. It was only a matter of time before she accepted her fate like everyone else.

The clock read five minutes until the end of the school day.

She whipped out her phone.

Perfect! How about 6?

Her heart dropped again when the message went from *delivered* to *read: 2:05 p.m.*

He's into me... and not too bad looking. She studied his photos for the hundredth time, trying to convince herself of the latter. *He just needs a clean shave—and new clothes.*

She found the thread of messages with her best friend, Clara.

Girl... I am going on a date tonight!!!

As she pressed send, someone let out a choking cough in the room, followed by a resounding, "*Ewww.*" An elementary school teacher's worst nightmare.

She looked up and saw Jonathan at the center of the group. He'd been shoving the flute as far up his nostril as it could go.

Now I have somewhat of an idea how the other two flutes broke...

—

Before she could leave for the day, Rhea had to take the recorder from Jonathan Yang and write a note for his parents stating that, although he seemed to enjoy recorder lessons, he was not using the instrument correctly and would no longer be allowed to participate. Any other teacher would've written him up for some kind of detention, especially since he'd been smart enough to manipulate her with those tears without revealing why he broke his last recorder. But Rhea didn't have the time, and she honestly didn't care enough.

She'd submitted her application to Julliard a few weeks ago, where she hoped to attend their doctorate program in music theory this coming fall. If she lost her long-term substitute teaching gig before that happened, so be it. She might miss out on cash in her pocket, but that would only give her more time to practice the violin. A part-time job sounded better, anyway, despite having to move back in with her parents.

Kids were storming out of the school and onto the buses when Rhea locked the door to her classroom. She shuffled out in the wake of children, attempting to sneak past the opened front doors, where two teachers stood watch on either side. Today there weren't only teachers seeing the students off, but Principal Overheem. Rhea felt his eyes arrowing on her, dissecting her intentions, and she had no choice but to acknowledge him with a wave. *You have to be kidding.* He had turned and started walking her way.

"Leaving so soon?" Overheem asked with one raised eyebrow, a wealth of condescension propelling the statement. Principal Overheem was one of four black faculty members in the school, and few of several in the district. The lack of minorities in Boise, Idaho irked Rhea all her life, making it a gut-wrenching task to step out of the house, into a world where everyone saw her as the other. Having Principal Overheem hold her to some ideal of a perfect young black woman inspiring students to be their best made her job unbearable. The slightest mistake was magnified and scrutinized by Overheem until she found herself asking to be excused from his office. A fact of life manifested itself so clearly in the principal's distaste for her. Sometimes the people most like Rhea were the ones dedicated to bringing her down.

They were two solid rocks, still against a flowing river of students. "I have a family emergency," she lied—good, too. Jonathan had nothing on her lying skills. It was how she got the job. "I'll be here early Monday morning to finish some grading." That also was a lie, but it was spoken through a performer's smile.

Overheem huffed, a big man that spent most of his days behind a desk, though his broad shoulders might have served some high school football team during his golden years. Perhaps that was why he held her to such a high standard. He didn't want her to strum the wrong chords and lead herself astray, like he did.

"And you'll be here tomorrow," he stated matter-of-factly. "For the faculty meeting. I'm confident you've prepared some thoughtful speaking points."

Rhea had a few speaking points that she wanted to share with Principal Overheem this very moment. Alas, she was not that careless, and still could use that paycheck. A twitch might have come over her face when she realized she had forgotten about the faculty meeting, but otherwise she remained calm.

She lowered her head as if mulling over an important point. "I have a few ideas to throw around. You'll see."

This brought a confident smile to Overheem's face. "I'd hope so. I always look forward to hearing what you have to say." With that, Overheem gave her a sort of insider's wink, and made his way back to the doors with his hands held behind his back.

After throwing open the exit doors, Rhea let out a deep breath—*mind over matter, mind over matter*. Faculty weren't supposed to park at the rear of the building, but she didn't like parking near anybody else because she didn't like speaking to anybody else. She didn't want to end up like them, so she didn't associate with them. It was like this with the person who occasionally went by the sobriquet, "best friend." Clara didn't do much in the creative realm—or any realm, for that matter—despite pontificating over ounces of weed she stole from her seasonal boyfriend's stash.

Rhea's phone buzzed as she entered the lonely car in the back parking lot—a blue Prius, sitting there like an expectant mother who came to pick up her child from the sleepover because she heard they were watching 'R' movies; a monster that sucked away anything even remotely cool.

She started the car with a press of the button and put her hands up to the warmer. Phone on her lap, she read the new message from Clara.

> *Oh my GoddDDD. GIRL. Okay, I have like twenty questions. Is he cute? What are you wearing? Where are you going? And why are we not sharing locations?*

Rhea couldn't help but smile while reading. Her phone vibrated and another message preview from Laird came, but she swiped it away. She'd been thinking of a reply to send to Clara. How could she say that Laird wasn't the hottest-looking man in the room, or the kindest, but at this point, she was willing to give basically anyone a chance? Part of her regretted messaging her friend in the first place.

—

What are you going to wear?

Rhea always taught in jeans and neutral-colored blouses. Wearing anything other than her bleak and sad ensemble made her feel like a soccer mom trying way too hard to prove she used to be hot. For the thousandth time, she cursed her lack of style as she sifted through beige, tan, and khaki tops, researching celebrity outfits on the internet and trying to copy them with her thrifted wardrobe.

If Rhea knew what Laird wanted in a girl, then maybe she could dress like her. She figured it'd be safe to shoot for that mythical border between head-turning slut and expensive prude. Again, she found herself at the mercy of a world she didn't understand—this one belonging to another sex.

I'm an other.

She stopped on a rose-pink dress that hung in an hourglass figure, crafted with the sole purpose of forcing her body into that stereotypical shape.

Does Laird want a woman he can show off to his friends or someone he can take home to Mommy?

Rhea didn't like the idea of wearing the pink dress, especially on a first date. The thirsty looks—no, *hungry*—were enough to keep her from considering it most evenings.

But tonight wasn't most evenings. Nobody would try anything with a gym bro by her side, as long as she could keep him from starting anything with them.

The payoff at the end of the night might be worth wearing the dress. Laird most certainly valued seeing a little skin more than he did good manners. *The desperation will make clear what I really want. Guys like girls who are direct, don't they?* The problem was that Rhea had no idea what she wanted, only a vague, distant vision of romantic goals that she'd see on Instagram. Surely her needs couldn't be as superficial as needing some dick.

Her hand drifted toward her bed, her phone, the screen soon displaying the Instagram page of *Llswole*.

A white dude who kept his body impeccably... well, swole, stared back at her with a face that looked like a mix between McConaughey and Owen Wilson. She clicked on the tab showing his tagged photos and, within a few seconds, knew the type of girl he found attractive. At least half of his tagged photos showed him next to his bros, drenched in smoky neon light, with some unidentified ass thrown on top of them.

She closed the Instagram app with disgust and tossed her phone back onto the bed. Clearly she'd been putting way too much thought into this. Swallowing her pride and sucking in the little bump of her stomach, Rhea snapped a picture of herself in the pink dress.

She never sent it to Clara.

—

She sent Laird a message when she got into her car. Rhea's desperate state inspired her to give into the hard-hitting, zero-foreplay flirtation that so many guys thought appropriate off the jump. She sent him the picture of herself in the mirror instead of Clara.

Laird's response read:

You look so fucking hot...

Part of her regretted sending the picture, as if promising sex when he had yet to cough up even a nice meal, especially since he didn't send a picture back. *At least he thinks I'm attractive. The eager ones always have some new moves to show you, if they don't finish in point-two seconds.* But she wasn't able to judge his attractiveness, which made her think he was hiding something. She gave him the carrot without any stick.

Thanks! I'm about to leave now. Are you on the way?

Rhea typed the bar's address into her GPS before pulling out of the driveway. Apparently, the bar turned into a nightclub after eight. In their texts she had agreed to stay and dance, waving a metaphorical middle finger at tomorrow's staff meeting.

The bar was about thirty minutes away. Her hands practically shook while driving, and she managed to miss an exit just thinking about different things she could say that would make her look like a complete idiot to this dude. For example, she knew nothing about the gym. Also, this dress was shorter than she'd ever been used to. What if she stood up and flashed everyone, or spread her legs a *twitch* too far after a few drinks?

Still, she kept driving despite the angst, catching another exit down the highway. Cardi B played through the speakers at a cruising volume and she stared forward, trying to get in the hoe mindset, because it'd been too many months to count since her last date, and goddamnit she would rather wear next-to-nothing than sit inside and watch The Office for another night, alone.

After finally finding a parking spot almost a mile down the road, she glanced at her phone to see four new messages from *Llswole*. The crying and sad-faced emojis weren't a good sign.

I'm so sorry babe...
I'm not feeling too hot.
Can I get a raincheck?
I know—

Rhea couldn't finish reading.

She threw her phone into the passenger seat and slammed her fists against the steering wheel, over and over and over again. Her right hand connected with the center console hard enough to send a tingling soreness up her forearm. If she kept going, she'd punch the fucking windshield to pieces.

Her eyes welled with tears but she refused to cry, almost to breathe. She wouldn't let this asshole make her shed a single tear. Instead, she looked down, at the skin on her thighs, exposed for everyone to see, and thought about how stupid she'd been.

Her phone vibrated again. She didn't want to look, failing to stop herself.

A new message from Carla:

You got this shit girl! Let me know how it goes, or if you need an emergency call.
I am here—

She thought about telling her best friend everything. But revealing her innermost turmoil to someone who seemed perfectly satisfied with their dating life seemed as embarrassing as showing her bank account to a millionaire. Instead, she whipped out of the parking lot and into a nearby liquor store. On a Friday night in rural Florida, there wasn't much to do but get drunk at home or go to the local high school football game. The liquor store buzzed with people eager to do both.

On her way inside, Rhea despised every thirsty look she was given, paired with nudges and whispers, though she managed to keep a straight face and stay on task. She kept an "absolutely done with it" expression on while grabbing two bottles of blackberry wine, totaling somewhere in the ballpark of twenty dollars; what she would have paid when *Llswole* inevitably asked her to split the bill.

Her bitch-face worked its charm all the way to the store clerk, a failed millennial in the realest sense. She had a hooked piercing in her nose, green hair, and probably hated the world as much as Rhea did right that very second.

Come to think of it, Rhea had a lot in common with the girl behind the register. The only difference might have been that Rhea masked it all, hiding her true feelings to appear normal. She didn't know if that was a good or a bad thing. There seemed to be some power gained in refusing to take part in this fucked up mess of a world.

But where did that mentality land this fine, young liquor store clerk?

Rhea held on to Julliard like she assumed a woman her age held onto a baby during biblical times. She certainly didn't see herself teaching for more than a year. What would she do after, if Julliard never called? Maybe she would pick up a gig at that local bar and try making it as an independent violinist. She'd play on the side of the street during holidays and earn measly cash, dying unknown and irrelevant.

"Thanks," she said, giving her best encouraging smile before taking her brown bag and walking through the automatic doors. Outside, a group of college guys, young enough to be questioned if they walked inside, started giggling as she passed.

Rhea clenched her fists so she wouldn't glare at them.

"She's actually fine as fuck."

Surprisingly, the ignorant comment boosted her confidence despite the bottles of wine she carried and planned to drink alone. Sure, the kids were gross, but at least she still was "fine." It was something.

The next comment, shouted loud enough for the whole parking lot to hear, made her want to be done with life.

"Hey..." Giggles and whispers. "Keenan likes black girls!"

The words punched her in the gut.

They're only kids, she reminded herself, wondering what the hell they were doing here in the first place. An older man walked by as she fumbled for her keys, scrunching his lips together and shaking his head, as if to apologize for the boys' behavior.

Rhea finally unlocked her car and slid in, more livid than petrified. She could still hear the boys laughing.

2

ONLY IF

In the dense forest outside of the walls of Shadow Hills, Aramis found himself most at home.

His process to reach the forest was an arduous one, but over the years it had become a sacred ritual. Like a smith taking the short walk to his anvil, or the architect to their drawing board, he had his trek to the forest.

First, he descended the male castle by his normal means—a rune-bearing shield with magnetic propulsion pushing at different strengths against the metal of the mines beneath him.

As soon as his shield touched the ground, Aramis would hide it in a nearby rock crevice and venture out to the nearest section of the wall, passing through the castle gardens illuminated with plant bulbs that soaked in sun rays during the day, emitting a soft blue hue that paired so well with the moonlight—only a small taste of home.

Upon reaching the wall, Aramis checked around him once more to make sure nobody was watching, then entered through a crack he'd created after learning a spell of natural magick, capable of splitting apart the inner makings of rock like a zipper.

Finally reaching his cultivated clearing in the forest, Aramis investigated the books he'd stashed since last arrival, making sure they were in the specific order he'd left them in. He double-checked the subtle glowing shrubs he'd stolen from the castle gardens, looking for footprints and bent stems, any sign that someone might have been here since his last visit.

None.

Clean, like he left it.

Aramis couldn't stop himself from running through the consequences of being caught outside castle walls, practicing magick as a male mage. The constant fear kept him careful and safe. With the magickal crafts and all of their branches strictly designated for female fae, Aramis had to spend his years learning in the forest's bioluminescent solitude, fearing the punitive hand of the council.

If only they knew how wrong they were...

But now wasn't the time for worrying. That could be done during class or even the opening ceremony for all he cared. This quiet time was sacred.

Excitement rose inside of him when he felt safe enough to sit down and open up one of the newest books in his collection. There was always a thrill that came with studying magick, partly because it had to be done in secret. The fact that mentors and the very structure of fae society deemed magick a *female* craft made him want to perfect every aspect of it simply to show that he could. Lucky enough, he loved magick and all of its subcrafts more than anything he'd ever done in life.

Over the years, he'd been decent enough at hiding his true passion, but with the tournament fast approaching, a true test of his skills in the four traditional male crafts—smithing, architecture, hunting, and alchemy—would reveal Aramis's lack of male skills in front of the entire kingdom. He dreaded that fast-approaching day more with every second, burying his face deeper in books stolen from the female castle in an effort to forget.

Typically, when the moon reached its highest point and its silver rays produced beings inside of the forest—natural walkers—Aramis would have a long and delightful talk with those beings. He'd made friends with them despite coming to realize they were projections of his mind onto the magickal qualities of the moonlight.

But tonight, he paid the beings and their sad songs no mind, preferring to use the moonlight to read.

—

On his way back from the forest, he glimpsed the first light of dawn. Aramis had doubts—doubts he'd kept in the back of his mind since qualifying day—and these doubts flared the closer the first tournament day approached.

He'd been inducted into the Tournament of Hearts by his parents, a wish of theirs that consisted of nothing more than their darling child becoming an example male with all of the necessary skills to "survive." In the back of his mind, Aramis knew they hoped he would become a mentor, or perhaps even king. But as Aramis gazed upon the two towers in the distance, imposing their rules on the rest of the walled kingdom below them, he knew he would never be king in a place like this.

Well... He supposed that he could, if the right scenario arose. If you asked his fellow male contestants, they would say he was one of the worst in the class, but he was still there, competing.

The problem was that Aramis didn't feel as if he'd been a useful male fae at all. He fulfilled a role, went through the motions of becoming a proper smith, but none of it was meaningful to him. Nothing felt like opening up a magickal textbook and learning how to manipulate the realm more than a sword ever could.

He made his way back into the garden between male and female towers and gazed at the latter tower with its signature side room, where the princess stayed while males battled for a spot next to her as king. After short deliberation, Aramis made his way to the side of the female castle.

He didn't need a shield to enter this castle, given his knowledge of splitting rock. After an inspection during his third year, Aramis realized that the protective rune surrounding the female castle didn't account for the souls of male fae, so he could enter various halls and walkways as he pleased, and did regularly, stealing new reading material.

He still remained quiet as he snuck through darkened halls, past servants who couldn't find a worthy female skill to compete in, but still desired to serve the castle—members of the Tablua Rasa. Their depressed gait wasn't hard to sneak past. They were lost in their thoughts whenever Aramis mistakenly made a loud noise, hardly looking up from their nightly task of cleaning the castle.

Down a winding staircase, he stepped into a room illuminated with violet light. The purpose of this room wasn't entirely clear, though everytime he would try to take another guess based on the latest book he'd acquired. Last time it was a book about summoning, but it was so complex, Aramis couldn't determine if it was under the branch of dark or conjuration magick, or perhaps both. From what he'd gathered so far, this room had to at least welcome the thought of dark magick. The shelved orb calling his attention from over his left shoulder was used to see prophecies—but one had to be careful with how they looked into the violet smoke, less they become obsessed with what they saw.

Or so Aramis read. He didn't risk a glance, choosing another book off the shelf at random—it didn't make much of a difference given his lack of knowledge—and heading back up the winding stairs. He dodged past servants not aligned with an arbitrary female skill, trying not to think too hard about what their fate was compared to his. He could've ended up just like them, sweeping floors in the male castle, if he hadn't been good enough at smithing to qualify for the tournament.

He felt cowardly. How long would he keep hiding his magickal interests in a world where others like him were forced to suffer? How long could he?

He remembered the first time he'd tried to show his magickal skills to his friends, their lack of reaction. They moved onto the next subject as soon as possible.

So he'd mentioned it in class, in front of everyone. Aramis wanted to note the presence of the female craft of natural magick when it came to smithing ore material, how it all seemed connected, each craft relying on one another, which eventually led to the idea that the crafts shouldn't be separated to begin with, but the smithing mentor made him sit out for the rest of the lesson.

After class, Sinisar spoke to Aramis in his authoritative tone about the negative effect of female crafts on the male mind, rendering males weak and unable to compete in the very games they trained to win. He pointed out the servants of the male castle as an example, other members of the Tabula Rasa, and how none of their meager figures could win the tournament, because they spent all day making things beautiful, rather than training.

When Aramis pointed out how the members of the Tabula Rasa didn't have a choice but to serve the castle after failing to qualify for a male craft, sacrificing their wings upon testing day for the good of the kingdom and taught to obey thereafter, Sinisar lectured about the necessary balance of masculine and feminine forces, and how males served a specific purpose for the kingdom that provided for them, and that purpose, according to the smithing guild, was to fight.

The smithing mentor then referred to the metaphor of a pendulum for the first time of many throughout Aramis's training years. He claimed Shadow Hills was in a current state of peace, inhabited by female forces, with the pendelum swinging far left. A frivoless and delightful time, he said, compared to the masculine forces that awaited the pendulum's momentum in the years to come. The other side of the pendulum was a necessary period of war in Sinisar's eyes, and who else to fight in that war but the trained male smiths? Apparently, Sinisar awaited that period gladly.

He'd then asked if Aramis had heard about the blood and light prophecy, but he'd heard of no such thing. From then on, Sinisar made sure Aramis had the worst time smithing.

Aramis still felt the hatred of that moment even while creeping up through the female staircase. If it weren't for fae like Sinisar, he wouldn't have to go behind the kingdom's back and steal books about magick.

At the top of the stairs, Aramis opened the door and fixed upon a violet light similar to the room he'd visited—except this light radiated from the earrings and nose stud of the dark mentor. She fluttered subtly through the halls, a nightgown trailing behind her like some sort of dark magickal power. Aramis couldn't help but wonder at the mesmerizing beauty of Celeste, whose eyes eventually turned to meet his.

His heart dropped, stepping back to close the door.

I'm done, he thought. *She's on her way to capture me, take me to the council, and that will be the end of any hope to compete.*

As the violet light shone brighter through the door's bottom gap, Aramis could hardly breathe. He didn't bother trying to run down the stairs. She'd seen him plainly.

But the light continued past him, gradually fading away.

For a long while, Aramis sat in the staircase, book tucked beneath his arms. Then he remembered that dawn was close, and being seen coming out of the female castle by other contestants might be worse than being turned into the council, on account of the ridicule.

—

Climbing back up the male tower was never much of an issue for Aramis, especially since he'd learned how to carve the magnetic rune of levitation. He always appreciated the logic of rune-crafting and its immediate feedback of success, and more often, failure. Rune-crafting didn't require brawn or chance, no waiting upon his opponent to make a mistake so he could slash them. Rune-crafting was a precise art, closer to alchemy, and it allowed for so much more than any male craft Aramis had ever known.

Another dark magick book hiked under his arm, he sat upon the shield he'd imbued with a magnetic rune and used it to propel himself to the window of his room in the castle.

He struggled through the window and slid the shield beneath his bed along with his new book, closing the window behind him and waiting, listening for anyone he might have alerted. He shouldn't have been out this late into the morning, but it was worth every second. It was the only time Aramis had to practice what he truly enjoyed. Any other time, he was simply doing what everyone else wanted him to do.

What would he do during the tournament, when he couldn't fake his skills or run away?

As he laid his head on the pillow, the future seemed bleak, and it gave rise to a fiery pain in his chest that couldn't be doused. He could either compete as a male contestant, performing terribly and hoping some female contestant saw enough potential in his skills to desire him as a mate...

Or he could renounce the tournament altogether, facing the consequences of his truth.

That would be the brave thing to do.

🌿 3 🌿

IMPRESSIONS

The next morning, Aramis woke up early—rather, he'd only napped for an hour at most—and he had a few moments before training began, which he used to read his newest book.

Today was the last training day before opening ceremonies commenced, and he knew it was going to be rough. It was a day when they would receive ranks based on their relative skills with smithing and combat. But Brok, the most respected smithing contestant simply because of his confidence and charm, had been talking to the class about how they had to prove their skills for the games coming up, showing the mentors that they're a "good batch" of smiths. They would have time to rest with the opening ceremony, he claimed, but today was when they were supposed to battle one another and prove their worth.

Aramis wanted to free his mind from worry with the practice of magick, but that didn't seem to be in the crystal ball.

He settled for his newest book, which wrote extensively on the topic of the blood and light prophecy. The book was a newer print despite the worn edges and annotations along nearly every line. Its pages turned with the stiffness of a book unread, though the stains on the sand-colored page told otherwise. Aramis couldn't blame the previous reader for not staving their hand, slightly sorry he took the book in the first place, as the prophecy was one of the most interesting things he'd ever read about regarding dark magick. It explained the nature of the kingdom in terms of balance better than Sinisar ever could, taking into account the role of the mentors, the king and queen.

It began with an explanation of the tournament:

The Tournament of Hearts was created during the first season of Shadow Hills at the behest of the first season's divine queen, Nepenthe. The Tournament was the final extension of her perfected ideal of the Shadow Hills realm—a kingdom where fae from all around the realm would come to learn classic fae skills and have a chance to become king or queen for a season.

Two castles were built upon the founding of Shadow Hills, one designated for females and one for males. The female castle was built to teach crafts reflecting feminine fae traits, all magickal in nature. The male castle was built to teach crafts reflecting masculine fae traits, all physical in nature. Contestants graduated within their given craft have a chance to compete in the Tournament of Hearts.

Female contestants are tasked with creating four different games that correctly test for skills in various male crafts. Male contestants then compete against one another in the games of the female creation. This way, the true desires of the female fae may be tested in the males, and the best may rise to the throne.

The male who displays the greatest skill of smithing will then become the smithing mentor for the next season, teaching future contestants. And so on for the remaining crafts. But the male with the greatest overall skill in every game is the tournament's winner, earning the hand of the Asenath.

Who is the Asenath, a newcomer to the kingdom may ask...

The Asenath is a newcomer herself, the term supposedly created by the first season's dark mentor, Samara. Sources tell of a hostile relationship between Samara and Nepenthe, two mentors of dark and divine forces holding our very realm together. Samara felt the tournament was much too rigid to produce beneficial kings and queens during future seasons, requiring a wild card of sorts.

Tension between the two mentors culminated in the creation of the first ever compass portal, a device meant to locate the most beautiful female in all the realms, taking into account the needs of the Shadow Hills kingdom and its current balanced state.

All this to say, the blood and light prophecy, seen with the very same prophetic magick as the compass portal, tells of a time when the portal will be cloudy and dysfunctional. Masculine forces are suspected to gain prominence within this period, bringing blood, and given the lack of dark forces, an utterly blinding—

"What are you reading?" A voice asked from the doorway.

Garrett.

Aramis closed the book and looked up, throwing it to the side of the bed. "Time to train already?"

His friend walked off, keeping the door halfway open. Aramis couldn't help but note how much his wings had grown in comparison to his own, expanding across his shoulders after sneaking through a slit in pearl white armor.

Aramis looked at his closet for something to change into, seeing two options that would define how his day went. He could wear armor and fit in with the rest of the smiths, or he could wear a mage's cloak, and stick out like a spoiled bladeleaf while standing up for the idea of fae practicing any craft they pleased.

"Time goes by quickly when you don't get any sleep." Garrett spoke as if there wasn't a hidden message in his words, always playing the nice fae.

Aramis halted while donning the black cloak, smooth enough to slip through his hands. "You knew I was out?"

"I don't know how the whole castle didn't know," Garrett's brother said—Kollin. They stayed in rooms opposite Aramis, sharing a collective lounge space that apparently carried sound rather well.

"I was out exploring," he said, hoping to put the topic to rest. Neither of them made eye contact as he made his way to the food cabinet and drizzled honey on a bowl of chickweed and stinging nettle.

"You better not get caught." Garrett's tone was somber. If Aramis looked now, his arms were probably crossed and he probably had a stern face. He meant well, but Garrett thought he knew what was best for everyone, mistaking himself for a father in a fatherless castle.

"Yeah..." Kollin said. "I don't want to be banned from the tournament for being around you."

Aramis clenched his fists, feeling his heartbeat quicken and palms break into a sweat. Kollin spoke as if he was the one taking the risks. "You won't get banned. It's not like it was your idea for me to do any of this."

"No? What about when they come to ask me if I knew if you were gone? If I knew about all this magick you do in quiet? What do I say then?"

"Lie," Aramis said, hoping for a second time to put the topic to rest with a bite of his breakfast, which he didn't want anymore.

Kollin looked at his brother, like he always did when losing an argument. "Look at what he's wearing? Brok is going to say something about his lack of armor."

"He's right," Garrett—the voice of reason—agreed. "I have another set in my room you can put on. It's a little small for me. It might fit you."

Aramis continued eating his breakfast in silence, refusing to acknowledge Garrett as he leaned next to him on the counter.

"We're just saying, we're worried about you."

Kollin stood from the table, as if being around Aramis was enough to get him banished from the kingdom. "Why should we be worried, when he doesn't even care about himself? He can't even take training seriously. I don't want to be around this."

"Don't be," Aramis said, taking another bite.

Kollin shook his head and left.

Garrett stood from the table, still lingering, his hand sweeping nothing off the wooden table infused with a sliver of moonstone. "You know, you don't have to—"

"I'll be fine."

Finally, everyone left and Aramis could crack open his new book and continue reading while he ate. It was hard to read, though. His attention revolved around the disappointed faces of his friends, and how he wished things could be different, so he wouldn't have to choose between them or the study of magick.

He wasn't even hungry, but he forced himself to finish every last bit of the sweet nettle. It was going to be a long day.

—

Aramis walked to the training arena alone.

Lost in thought about the blood and light prophecy, he hadn't noticed the crowd of female contestants gathered around to watch the smith's final day of training until hearing their delightfully high voices. The female contestants stood along the arena's low wall, while villagers stood out further, past the invisible barrier placed between them and the contestants. Nearer to the arena, in a glass box floating high above the sand with the help of multiple runes, the mentors watched with subtle nods and smirks from jokes the lesser fae couldn't hear.

Aramis's heart dropped at the thought of having to fight in front of so many eyes. *Should I use magick?* It would be impossible to win if he didn't, but with so many people watching, he knew of no discreet spell that would cause any real damage.

If he was seen doing magick, what would they think? He knew the males would start saying he shouldn't compete. Even now, everybody looked at him as he joined the group of smiths, wandering in their cliques. They scanned up and down his mage's cloak as he passed.

Kollin and Garrett were a thankful sight, leaning with their arms over the fence and looking out to the arena at the current fight. Aramis almost grasped Kollin's shoulder to say hello, then remembered they probably didn't want to be seen with him. He walked a bit further down the fence, still within talking distance, and it was Kollin who spoke first.

"You going out there today?"

"I don't know why I wouldn't." Aramis ignored the casual glance Kollin made at his cloak.

"I think what my brother is trying to say," Garrett corrected, "is that you're going to get weird looks."

"Too late." Out on the dirt arena, Aramis watched sand and debris fly into the air as someone took a wooden sword to the arm, thus defeated.

"And you're not ashamed?" Kollin asked. "Not even a little bit?"

The next name was called to fight—Brok. It would be interesting to see how one of the best smiths handled the last day of training. Aramis glanced at the mentors perched inside of the arena box, always separated from the contestants. They gathered near the window, much more attentive to Brok compared to the contestants before him.

Aramis felt a shove at his side.

"Stand back, mage. And nice dress." A deep chuckle from the hearty gut of Brok as he jumped over the fence, armor clinking loosely on his shoulders. He never wore the best armor, as if he didn't much care about looks, but that made him even more intimidating. He defeated his opponents with sheer skill.

"Move aside, female," shouted one of Brok's friends, Zane, met by a healthy roar of laughter. "I can't see."

Aramis lowered his head. He thought is best to avoid retaliation and move closer to Kollin and Garrett.

"How long are you gonna let them talk to you like that?" Kollin asked.

"He's gonna get back at them in the tournament," Garrett answered, shooting a side-eye at Aramis before turning to watch Brok fight. He'd been second behind Brok in nearly every training session.

"Isn't that right?" Garrett went on. "I have to assume that's why you've been sneaking out at night. Trying to find some sneaky mage way to make it through the tournament. At least, I hope you came up with something."

Sneaky?

Aramis knew his friend didn't mean to refer to the few magickal expeditions he savored as if they were a rat's escapade. He knew he didn't mean to have such a condescending tone, or rule out the fact that Aramis had any chance of winning if he fought like a normal male smith.

But could he blame him?

This tournament, this week, Aramis would have to prove himself in front of everyone, like he so miserably had during his qualifying dual, when he tripped his opponent with the use of a last-minute conjuring spell. He certainly resorted to sneaky magick back then. Would he have to once more?

Maybe he hadn't learned as much from the books as he thought. Aramis found he could explain the structure of the fae council—every mentor the best of their season, the king being the pinnacle and queen from another realm, keeping the kingdom's balance true—but how could that help him win?

He counted all eight of the mentors through the glass, and the king standing solemnly near the back. With all the talk of the blood and light prophecy, he couldn't help but note the queen's absence. If the prophecy was true, then the queen's absence had significance given the swing back into forces of the male castle. War, according to Sinisar. Blood, and light.

It was as if the divine queen stood by the king in solemnity, draped in her golden silk robe, a winged crown adorned over burnt blonde braids. The text spoke of the Asenath's importance in keeping the masculine and feminine forces equal, like the corrective force of a pendulum, according to Sinisar. If they were currently in a state without a queen at all, did that mean masculine forces would drive the kingdom without correction?

"Don't you guys find it odd the queen isn't here with everyone else?"

Kollin gave him a wide-eyed stare. "He's doomed."

Garrett winced as Brok flipped his opponent. "Aramis isn't hopeless. He's just... misunderstood." He pursed his lips at the glass booth —the way he and Kollin pointed at everything, supposedly a result of growing up in the tribes of Komuta, where smiths were bred like cattle. "Maybe the queen had the same idea as you, and would rather practice magick than watch a boring fight."

"Thanks," Aramis said, "but I doubt it. When was the last time you saw the queen doing any magickal work? The mentors are the ones who—"

"The next contestant is Aramis, seed fifty-seven." Their seed reflected their rank in the smithing guild, by the judgment of the smithing mentor, Sinisar. There were only fifty-seven contestants in his guild.

Murmurs arose that Aramis had no trouble trying to ignore, given the thousands of spells he was running through in his head, searching for anything with low visibility and high effect. But he'd only been studying the basic things that could take down an average opponent. He wasn't trying to be sneaky, though maybe he should've embraced his stereotype.

"Let's go," Brok said, jumping back over the fence. He'd broken a sweat defeating his opponent, but his breathing was steadier than Aramis's. "You're up, big guy."

"The opponent contestant will be Zane, seed twenty-three."

An eruption of applause and early congratulations arose from behind Aramis. A smile grew on Brok's face. "Look at that? One of my own." His pat on Aramis's back almost sent him careening into the fence.

He took a deep breath. Kollin and Garrett refused to look back at him.

While jumping the fence, his foot caught on the highest post, sending him tumbling face-first into the dirt arena. The resulting laughter was almost louder than Brok's cheer. It was like everyone felt they could laugh at him because of his mage cloak. He would never be taken seriously anymore.

"I can't watch," Kollin said as expensive armor clinked away.

Maybe I should display my skills with magick, he thought, walking toward the center circle. *Just to show I'm not a complete dunce*. He could cast a simple lightning spell given the texture of the clouds—he'd been paying attention to such a thing after stealing his Introduction to Naturalism textbook. It would be so satisfying to watch Zane convulse from all of the energy. *Let's see him try to laugh then*. How desperately he wished he could at least flaunt the maturity of growing wings.

A glance at his opponent reminded him to make his way to the sword cart, almost having forgotten a weapon to duel with. The inscription on the shed overhead, slashed repeatedly with wild sword throws, read, "A smith must test their creations."

Aramis could hear both male and female fae still laughing as he made his way out to the arena's center. His training sword, made of oak and reinforced along the edges with bent silver, weighed heavy in his hand. Much heavier than any spell would weigh upon his fingertips.

I could defeat him with a simple magnetic rune... I could carve it into the sword now, while nobody is looking.

But the runic glow would draw attention. Using magick for all to see would be even worse than losing the combat duel. It'd be admitting his refusal to serve the kingdom and give up his wings, like a good fae. They would believe him to think himself better than everyone else, capable of breaking sacred tradition without consequence, testing the balance, and as Sinisar once put it, "disrespecting the sacred forces at work."

For now, Aramis had to pretend he knew nothing about magick and only had a slight interest in cloaks. He had to pretend he respected the sacred forces, even though they provided him with nothing but pent-up secrets and a missing queen. Another glance at the mentors before the fighting began, before he inevitably lost, and at the sight of the Sinisar's disapproving gaze, all of his worries felt exposed.

✢ 4 ✢
FAERY INSTINCTS

Training ended with Aramis in the dirt, his cloak torn and eventually thrown away when he returned back to his room in the male castle. He hated that this was only the beginning of the tournament's festivities encroaching upon everything he knew and loved about his secret life, but tonight's event wasn't so bad. He cleaned himself up, putting on the best mage robe he could find and even some light armor over it. Tonight he wouldn't be able to practice magick, but he perhaps had the next best thing—dining next to female mages.

When he was finished getting ready, he looked out the window to see other smiths gathering on the steps in front of the castle with male contestants, females doing the same on their castle's steps opposite the garden. He would rather hit himself in the head with a hammer than join the others in front of the castle, turning to his book, reading until the last possible moment before he had to leave for the feast...

The dark mentor of long ago, Samara, was ingenious in her portal invention. She had studied fae history, the fae mind, but more so, acted as any true dark mage would, and foresaw times when the kingdom would shift. Samara, wise in her ways, knew the music of the fae soul and played a tune that told her of the realm's needs. It is said that very tune, like a humming lullaby, still plays around the portal to this day.

The kingdom's strict commands to keep males and females apart signaled trouble for the mentor, who knew fae souls all too well. Because the king and queen are models for the kingdom, she crafted a portal that would search the realms for a queen who fit the exact needs of the kingdom, to be reflected in the kingdom's citizens. When bonded with the king, the kingdom will find a way to heal and live to see a new season.

As seasons continue, one can see the blood and light prophecy beginning to bury its tendrils into the kingdom's foundation, its musical patterns telling us all we need to know. Discordant notes are being played in the constant deterioration of the kingdom's lower district, creating a harsh, depressing melody. The mentors grow more distant from those they are meant to teach, sometimes hearing a different song entirely. I fear their song is one of separation and disgust.

The purpose of this book, to end this prolonged introduction, is to ask, what might one need to do to stave the momentum of male forces as they career back into the kingdom, given the signs of the blood and light prophecy? Is there anyone with the foresight of Samara to tell?

———

The female conjurer moved so elegantly, she caught Aramis by surprise. He couldn't help but allow his gaze to drift across the banquet table, nearly flinching at the gentle smile shot his way.

He froze. Beads of sweat erupted on his palms and forehead. He'd never been under such a potent spell, cast so effortlessly.

In literal terms, he was not frozen, but moving along the banquet line stiffly, following his fellow smiths. Gold plates were stuffed to the brim with vegetables and tart cakes, and many sweet liquids and jams jiggled in dazzling containers. A steady hum of conversation filled the ancient hall, creeping up pillars of stone to an overlooking porch, on which the mentors lived their separate lives.

For Aramis, the world had fallen quiet. He placed none of the honeyed vegetables on his tray, and didn't dare raise his head again unless it was to cherish the female fae's beauty from across the table.

The mentors would certainly condemn any flirtation before the tourna-

ment... before the king was chosen and his soul was paired. But weren't males and females here to dine with one another for the first time since training began? And what was the point in doing so, if they could not merely converse?

Granting the matter no further thought, Aramis donned his most pleasant smile, and reached for the spoon she'd returned to the bowl of beets.

"These are my favorite," he said from across the buffet table, sensing the stupidity in his words as they were leaving his mouth.

The surrounding fae fell silent. Not a single being reached for more food, less the conjurer reply, and they not hear. The hot gaze of a crowd fell over him. Aramis seemed to have broken the unspoken rule of limited speech.

Her responding giggle spread like song throughout the room.

They walked in unison, tethered by their courage to make eye contact—her eyes a stunning ruby hue—and smile, practically floating toward the end of the banquet table. He felt as if a beam of precious light carried him forth. The table's end came too soon. He looked down to see hardly any food on his plate—more pressingly, he could only steal one final glance as the conjurer topped off her canteen from one of many gilded carafes at the end of the line.

Before turning, she smiled at him once more, and Aramis felt her spell enter his bones. He was at her command.

He remained listless as she ambled away—though inside, an aching, burning heat spread throughout his chest. And at the sight of her leaving, Aramis felt a part of himself break for the first time.

—

"She was into you," Kollin said, neglecting the meal in front of him. Tall candelabras danced through the air above them providing a warm, flickering light, under which they could feast. But utter disbelief possessed his friend. His look—wide-eyed and mouth agape—implied he would be doing *so* much more if he were in Aramis's position right now. "If you're too frightened to go and talk to her—"

"Do you understand how stupid that sounds?" Garrett, ever the older brother, glared up from his food.

He was two years the senior, though often mistaken for a twin when the brothers stood side-by-side. They even had similar markings on their faces, tattooed in faded blue ink; the shape of two moons faced one another, only full when the brothers stood side-by-side. The marks ran from the bottom of their chin to the middle of their forehead, and apparently, were their father's idea.

"He will draw the attention of every being in here," Garrett went on. "Do you want to be banned from the tournament before it begins?"

"He's right," Aramis said over the lunch and conversation. "Don't get me wrong, she's indescribable. Looking at her makes my heart race... but if we were caught together, I'd lose all chances of becoming king. The mentors would never let me compete." Even as he spoke, Aramis heard his lack of enthusiasm. "Besides..." He would try to convince himself. "I don't think she was flirting with me."

The precious smile she threw his way made this last statement feel like an outright lie. *Who am I fooling?...* he thought. *The realm can't possibly go on if I do not see her smile again.*

But could she have been flirting, inviting him to know her, or did she enjoy making him nervous because it bolstered her ego? Perhaps she knew that nothing could possibly emerge from the fire between them, but found amusement in adding kindling, and watching the fire grow.

"My fellow fae... If that's what you think, I'd have to say you are blind." Kollin leaned closer to the table, surveying all fae within a two-seat vicinity. "What do you guys think?"

The group nodded and gave encouraging winks while elbowing one another. Apparently, they'd seen her flirting as well.

Aramis looked straight down, cheeks radiating heat. The part of him that wanted to see where such a conversation would lead felt inevitable. He couldn't keep his foot from tapping, palms leaving blots of sweat against the polished wood table.

"What good would come of it?" Garrett asked him. "No bonds are to be established until *after* the tournament. We are not to interact with female fae. Can the rules be any clearer?"

Groans and objections came from the surrounding seats. Garrett, apparently, also was a coward and a bore.

And yet, in Aramis's humble opinion, the rule did seem to be another meaningless tradition.

Why keep the towers apart for so long, when its inhabitants are expected to spend their lives together? Would it not be best for them to know one another intimately?

They'd have a better understanding of each other's crafts, interests, and behaviors. Aramis would know if the female conjurer might react positively to his reaching out. What a detestable position the mentors put him in, risking his future if he pursued a curious passion.

"Don't listen to them," Garrett said. "Be patient and wait your turn. After the tournament. Who knows... you could win and become king?"

"I could? Me... A *male* mage?" Aramis laughed. "That's news to some."

"See! This one knows the truth about himself." The phrase wasn't spoken as a compliment, but rather, like the observation of a rare creature, and it came from several seats down the table, from Brok— a friend of Garrett's who, as Aramis realized over the years, had a deep appreciation for the combative life. "Cut him a break. He's a male mage, preferring books and pleasant spells over the noble life of a warrior. You can't expect him to have any *real* courage. Whether it be on the battlefield, or with the other sex."

This garnered indulgent laughter. Aramis leered at Brok from across the row of seats. Brok's constant jokes about the feminine qualities of the magickal arts, along with his insistence upon dying in battle, led Aramis to assume he resented the presence of a male mage hiding under the guise of a sub-par warrior.

Over their years of studying in the smithing guild, Brok drifted into a different friend group. This new group made their dislike for mages apparent by openly criticizing female practitioners, who they claimed did nothing for the community but "make things look nice."

Though Aramis saw the value in beauty and aesthetics, and the power of such forces to sway the kingdom's mood, he also knew that magick served as one of the vital pillars keeping the kingdom operational. The practice ran much deeper than Brok's simplified version of base-level alchemy—which, to Aramis's pleasure, Brok had failed repeatedly. It was interesting to see how such a fae took the very tower he lived in for granted. The concept of a towering, twin-thin building would've been near impossible to achieve if it weren't for the insight of reinforcing stone with sap conjured from another realm, filling the tiniest gaps with a substance harder than crystal.

Brok and the rest of the lowly smiths didn't understand the magickal arts, and that would've been okay, if they didn't condemn it. They only cared about how they could use metal in and outside of the forge. They did not think about the future or well-being of the kingdom, but of glory and what would pleasure them most.

A selfish, single-minded, and narrow sort of thinking. Aramis had come to realize the caring breadth a craft like dark magick had to offer. Why study how to wield a sword, when he could sway the hearts of warriors with a prophecy?

"You think this cowardice is humiliating?" Brok went on. "Wait till you see how he begins to cry during the tournament."

Kollin struck the table and made an attempt to stand, though Garrett pulled his brother down one-handedly, without looking up from his food.

"This is not our fight," Garrett said.

A long moment passed, during which the younger brother stared at Aramis with his arms crossed. The single, powerful emotion of hatred crackling across his entire being with shaky, direct movements. "You're going to let him talk to you like that?"

Aramis was going to say no, but could he retaliate with any real effect? What would be the point? A short quibble at the table?

He shook his head, letting the table's attention dissipate away from him.

If he did prove Brok wrong, it would need to be subtle. His courageous act of speaking with the conjurer would have to sneak under the mentor's eyes, while appealing to Aramis's magickal strengths... something cunning and impressive. He'd have to speak the conjurer's language.

He glanced up at the balcony where mentors of every craft overlooked their students, the upcoming contestants. The perfect idea popped into his mind, rather obviously, but would he have the courage to do it? It seemed poetic, truly; he'd been studying conjuration magick as of late.

The mentors seemed preoccupied with food, drinks, and gossip within their circle. Aramis reminded himself often that they were fae too, with basic desires and basic fears. When the mentors gave speeches, they put on faces of triumph and responsibility, wearing dresses made of luscious vines that wrapped up and around their perfectly defined legs—Aramis easily grew distracted. Or they wore dueling armor of the most rare, oddly-crafted quality.

But in his wiser times, Aramis paid attention to simpler things: the way the mentors spoke to one another, and how they laughed with open eyes and reserved smiles, or with their heads tilted back in delight. The mentors were not so courageous when speaking to individuals in the same hierarchy as themselves. Their desire to appear powerful was either shot down with a flaming arrow or charmed away by others just as powerful as themselves. At those times, like on the balcony now, Aramis noticed nervous sways and lingering touches.

The mentors were normal fae...

Just like the conjurer.

She smiled at you. Do you need any more of an invitation?

His heart pounded in his chest, foot tapping once more as he positioned his hands in a precise form beneath the table.

Over his lap, he had his left hand atop the right, both with the pointer finger and thumb extended. *"Nuntius,"* he uttered. Looking around the table, everyone seemed to have forgotten about him.

He glided the top of his left hand over the top of his right, and his tongue went fat with nerves as a paper note appeared encased inside of a red protective lining, keeping any substance from another realm from infecting that of the fae.

He gulped. The note continued to expand along with the moving border of his fingers.

Kollin sharply inhaled. His eyes felt like huge lanterns to the self-concious Aramis, casting their light on his hands beneath the table.

Aramis realized he'd been smiling, practically laughing to himself. Kollin's reaction made it even more worthwhile. So would Brok's.

By the time Garrett looked beneath the table, Aramis had thought the note away.

But not too far. Only toward the table directly across from his own, where the beautiful horned fae sat laughing with her friends.

Is it possible she already forgot me?

The note must be on their table now. She *must* be repulsed by how forward he'd been. And what if the note didn't even go to her table, but to the mentors?

He dismissed useless thoughts with an exhale, as the textbook advised him to do. "Conjurers must maintain a clear, focused mind while working," wrote the female author. "Distraction does not benefit those who wish to connect one dot to another." The essence of conjuration magick: connectivity, and one's ability to frame space and time so that one position seems identical to the other, if only for a mere moment. He remembered thinking of the possibilities till the sunset.

But more possibilities meant more potential for mistakes. The feel of the note was still slightly rough in his hands, despite existing at another position in the realm. Now, what to say? His message had to be polite, and obviously directed toward the one girl who smiled at him.

He smelled the humid air; seeing the conjurer smile was like seeing the sunset for the first time.

He closed his eyes, scratching the message out as a mental picture in his head. As the textbook instructed, he envisioned the words with the brightest coloring he possibly knew.

What is the penalty for pursuing a smile? I'm willing to risk it for yours.

Suddenly, his palms were empty. He opened his eyes to see Kollin and Garrett staring back at him.

He looked around, hoping the note reached the correct table. Nobody reacted so far. Judging by the quiet, completely normal state of the lunch hall, the note made it somewhere out of the castle entirely.

Perhaps he'd been too inconspicuous.

A chorus of sing-song laughter erupted from across the opposite side of the hall. The sound made every male turn their head. Aramis hoped he was right in thinking it came from the conjurer's table, and wasn't a mocking sort of laughter, but an excited one, igniting jealous envy in her friends.

Fae closest to him turned with their own mischievous, jealous smiles. As if Aramis, the mage, couldn't possibly have been the catalyst for that beautiful sound.

All except Brok, who chewed his bottom lip, glaring out toward the opposite tables.

After the initial wonder and intrigue, clinks from dishes and silverware could easily be heard as they awaited repercussions. Aramis clinched every muscle and hardly touched the insignificant food pile on his plate.

But the punishment never came. Few fae spoke at the male tables. Aramis stole an occasional glance toward the balcony, where mentors dined and talked in an incredibly friendly fashion. Goblets raised and clinked often.

As time went on and the conversations remained murmurs throughout the room, Aramis couldn't help but wonder whether he'd gone too far. Now that the taboo was broken, he himself an outcast, the realm would make an example out of him. It was only a matter of time before he was caught and punished.

And yet, it would be worth it. The chiming sound of her laughter would carry him through whatever punishment the mentors had in mind. They wouldn't throw him out of the tournament for such petty flirtation, would they? *I was only adoring her. Giving a compliment,* he could see himself pleading as the mentors cast him out past the kingdom's safe walls.

Luncheon soon ended, signaled by the groups of servant fae rising from their seats, who then split equally toward the two sides of the room. Their silver gowns added a certain darkness to the somber candlelight, supporting, if not adding to their steady movements. Triangular holes stood out in the rear torso of their otherwise concealing gowns, displaying scarred backs, from when the servants sacrificed their wings.

Perhaps mutilation was the fate that awaited Aramis. He thought back to the days of sorting, when he'd barely qualified to enter the guild of male smiths after battling and defeating his opponent through his understanding of a lesser-known craft. Nobody noticed his subtle use of elemental magick, as far as Aramis knew, but their eyes did raise when his foe tripped for the seventh time on a growing vine.

Fae that did not pass any test for any guild attended a separate induction ceremony, in which they swore their allegiance and abstinence, vowing to serve the kingdom as a member of the noble Tabula Rasa. They gave their souls to the kingdom and in return, became anew.

The Tabula Rasa of the male tower made their way out, walking in united pairs of two and forming a long row. The act seemed practiced. As they walked, they gathered plates in a growing stack that would've toppled over if it weren't for the enchantment, like a purple tube, growing its translucent sides higher as they stacked the dishes and utensils.

Mentors soon descended on the wind of their wings and aligned at the end of their respective craft's table, leading the male and female fae out of the dim hall. Aramis's smithing group was the second to leave. As he stood, he noticed the conjurer had nearly walked out of the opposite door.

Aramis remained quiet and faced forward. He couldn't afford any more attention, and would likely melt if she were to be smiling at him again, unable to resist the urge to profess his love.

Anxiety made his legs shake as he moved. His breath shortened and a light, tugging sensation came from his chest. Feeling the inside of his cloak... the tug came from his pocket.

Instead of telling anyone what might have been expertly placed inside of his cloak, he chose to let the excitement boil until he exited the hall, walked up the spiral staircase, said a short goodbye to Kollin and Garrett at the forty-second floor, and finally, ventured to his room on the eightieth.

For a moment, he stood there in the height of the male castle, looking out over the emerald tops of the kingdom's buildings—gems powered the city from their ability to store years of sunlight. He'd once thought Shadow Hills a place filled with dreams as grand as the castle that nurtured them. Now, he couldn't wait to compete in the tournament, even if he did lose. As a mage, he likely stood no chance of winning a game designed for testing the traditional male crafts of smithing, hunting, architecture, and medicine.

Nevertheless, he would try. And if he did win, then he would change the rules of the tournament forever. But when he lost, he wouldn't be hurt. Long ago, he'd accepted nothing much would amount from his life. Nothing could. His fate was to suffer practicing a craft that others already mastered, discovering what they already knew, working and working to perfect a spell with no real purpose other than to bring him, and those who might benefit from the spell, joy. Such a fate didn't seem like suffering, so much as playing. He loved perfecting his spells more than anything. And becoming a mage was a decision he made long ago.

He used to think he was less than the ale-sipping warriors that surrounded him. Never had his interest peaked near a sword. The others told him to give up in so many different ways; pressing his face up near the smelter, or throwing the week's latrine waste into his bedding.

But as his hand drifted toward whatever lay inside his cloak pocket, he felt he'd won. The fragile paper meant he'd been chosen by this female over the other males around him. Even Brok.

He tasted the alluring desire to be desired—the conjurer bolstering his ego—and he wanted more of it.

A floral scent seeped through the red, protective shield that surrounded the note. Elegant letters decorated the small paper's upper half. Images of the female fae rushed back to him.

He fell to his bed, sighing at the now realized scent of his love. Her angelic movements filled his mind. The note's contents repeatedly gave under the weight of his steaming, adoring imagination. He eventually managed to bring himself into focus by muttering the words as he read.

How sweet of you. My smile is the result of your bravery. Would you continue this courageous streak and visit me at the gardens this evening?

- S

Aramis couldn't help but pace around the room. Thoughts about the consequences of getting caught terrorized him—potential wing-lessness for the rest of his life. This wasn't as harmless as conjuring a little note. Then again, he had nothing more than stumps. Considering his stolen stack of magickal scrolls and texts, he'd already taken enough risks in his years of study to be suspended a hundred times over. Why stop now?

He waited for the moon to rise. Opening the window, Aramis basked in light shining up at him from the gardens; trees beaming a ghostly white with their sun-charged leaves.

What will I say when I see her?

It better come to him in the moment. If only his mentors had taught him how to go about meeting a female, he wouldn't have to worry about ruining her perception of him. *Will it be any different than meeting a male fae?* The answer seemed to be in his question. Like every-thing else, he had to go about this obstacle alone.

Thankfully, his shield was still propped against the side of his bunk. *There is one tool the smiths got right.* He wasn't going to use it to block any attacks today.

Aramis propped the shield, handle side up, onto the ledge of the open window. He took a deep breath and climbed into the disc, teetering out, anticipating the force that would push up against him. He'd decorated the shield with a magnetic rune, set to vary its strength and propel him at certain heights over the ground. A lever he installed at the side lowered him to the garden's glow, as if he fell into a dream, and he thumped against the ground with a force that made his teeth chatter. One final glance up at the castle wall made him question every action up to this point.

He forgot to close the window.

✻ 5 ✻
OLD WAYS

All of the anxious worries about what to say and how to act soon came to rest when he spotted the conjurer wandering alone in the gardens. Fluorescent blue leaves drenched her calculated movements in an alluring glow. A subtle knocking sound came from the bulbs of the garden's plants, striking a continuous *thrum-thrum-thrum,* setting a pace to their dance.

She drifted left, weightless as the leaf she inspected, reaching out and rubbing it with her thumb when she turned to him as if having discovered his presence long ago.

He did not—could not—move as she approached him the way someone might approach a cold drink in the desert—wide-eyed and *wanting*.

What was so wrong about this?

Her eyes bore into him, capable of revealing any truth. She increased her pace with every step. Aramis saw that her beauty wasn't only in her deliberate actions or ruby eyes like gleaming crystals; a visible aura surrounded her, a pink cloud, filled with the most disinhibiting scent unlike anything he'd ever known. The cloud encapsulated him and he never wanted to escape.

She grabbed his hands, staring up at him; ruby gems glinting in the moonlight. Celestial beauty reflecting through her own.

But he was weakened, fingers shaking and palms damp with sweat. The touch of a female fae had never been anything more than a fantasy. Abstract like convoluted spells. He could hardly believe the conjurer stood before him, touching him, gazing up with such intensity —such invitation—giving him the suggestive smile that started everything, though now she seemed so sure of herself.

The conjurer pulled him closer with hands softer than velvet, as if tired of waiting. Their hands clasped one another in an odd, bent position at their waist. He couldn't help but steal glances at the sight of her gown strap venturing off her right shoulder.

His hands drifted to her hips, a movement as natural as breathing. Any remaining nerves would soon be replaced by the intensity of foreign moments—a new realm they would soon explore together.

"Simmia..." she said. "And you are?"

"Aramis."

His mind then settled into a rather absolute calmness, a jovial idealism that coated all the realm in infinite possibility.

Starlight blessed them as they walked to the female castle, up and through its stairs as if Simmia were allowed to leave at any time of night.

They entered her room unnoticed. She pointed Aramis to the bed, where he sat while watching her wave over the walls and door, tracing paths for subtle orange flames that drifted to the ceiling and left behind a clear, filmy residue. The flames—strands of vermillion dancing with one another—emitted no heat. Aramis thought he'd recognized a pattern in the light's movement above him when a cautious, gliding touch began to move warmly up his knee...

Up his thigh...

Simmia knelt before him, next to the bed, and he froze. Her other hand touched his other knee. Now both hands moved slowly toward his inner thighs, where he had never felt so sensitive.

He held his breath.

The fact that they weren't supposed to be together granted their kisses and caressing infinite meaning. They were rebels, fighting against a law they believed to be ridiculous. And it felt otherworldly. The two of them moved as one.

When the fire between them calmed, the conjurer's decorative ceiling lights drenched the room in hues mimicking the seascape. His muscles tingled as he lay dazed, watching rivers of water-colored light swirl overhead. Tangled sheets constricted him. Sweat cooled on his skin. Night turned to early morning and the worries of brighter daylight came with it. He could only stay a moment longer.

Thinking of what to say became very difficult. How could it be, after they had shared such intimacy? It didn't seem possible to get closer to another being than he had with Simmia. Yet, a part of him still feared her judgment.

"If I'm here any longer, the council will know," he said. When she made no reply, he gestured toward the window. The sky provided a rose-pink background for thick, puffy gray clouds. "It's almost morning."

He removed his arm beneath the small of her back, standing with subtle hesitation. It took him too long to find his cloak on the ground amidst scattered sheets; he'd been searching so nervously. She would read his anxious energy and think he didn't enjoy their shared time.

While putting on his cloak, he waited for her to say... anything. If she gave any indication of wanting to prolong their time he would've yielded. That seductive cloud around her seemed to have a lingering effect. From this distance, Aramis still felt pulled by desire.

She shrugged her shoulders—previously draped over Aramis as she struggled to catch her breath. "It's easy to lose track of time with you."

"Are you hinting at something?"

"Hinting?" She tilted her head slightly, keeping eyes like heated coals set on him. When he didn't respond, she sighed and started fluffing the sheets around her. It seemed she was hinting at something. "Do I give you hope this kingdom will change?"

"Hope?" Aramis repeated, pretending to consider the question. He hated the idea of hope. Hope kept the dreamer from acting, filling their mind with ideas instead of prompting them to act. It was the truest downer. "I suppose I've thought of ways the kingdom could improve. Our sorting system is arbitrary. Males are limited to a certain set of crafts, females another. This might easily be changed, but the council believes such a system provides balance to the kingdom. Order. And if the balance is shifted..." He didn't see the need to outline those consequences. She knew well enough that males practicing outside their given crafts were thought to bring days of impenetrable darkness. "But I have little hope about changing the views of everyone in the realm."

How much did she know about his situation? Of course, she knew he practiced magick, because of the note, but did she know about the rejection he'd experienced? The need to hide his true interests from the world for the sake of living a normal life?

Simmia rolled sideways on the bed, and he drank in the sight of her curves and bare skin, the blanket slipping off of her. "Thinking is different than hoping... Yes?"

Aramis turned over the words in his head, mostly distracted. He had to look away but found it impossible, coming to one main conclusion about himself: the beauty of female fae greatly fascinated him.

She rolled again to her back, large breasts leaning on either side of her chest. "You are thinking too much. Use my life as an example. I came to Shadow Hills on a scholarship to study conjuration. Had I ever conjured anything before my arrival? No."

Aramis felt it unnecessary to hide his outburst of laughter. This had to be a joke. "That's impossible," he said, quickly realizing she wasn't laughing. But it didn't make sense to him. Shadow Hills recruited tournament contestants based on skills alone. "How did you make it through evaluations?"

"I could ask the same of you," she said.

"I'm different. You've never seen me fight. I'm quite good." He lied with a sense of false confidence that made the effects of her aura quickly dissipate. The distance between them suddenly felt greater even though he didn't move a step, allowing more room for further disagreement.

"Did you think this was a show?" she asked, looking to the cyan lights above her. "It is a barrier, blocking sound from leaving this room. Beyond your level of magickal knowledge, yes?"

He swallowed, feeling humiliated. And her calling out his lack of knowledge made him angry. "All right. Then how did you get the scholarship?"

Simmia pointed to the tip of her thin nose, accented by the high set of her cheekbones. "That's the question I asked many years ago, though in a different form. How *would* I get a scholarship? I heard this was the land of a thousand gems. *A miner's paradise.* Music to the ears of a little colonist far, far away from the Hills." Perhaps, in her village, everyone had the same garnet hair, thick and voluminous after their time in the sheets.

"You came here for smithing..." The dots started to connect. Simmia didn't fit the mold for typical female crafts. Her personality matched perfectly with that of a miner—tough people willing to venture into the darkness with no more than a pickaxe and a broadsword. Since they'd met, she hadn't shown much emotion other than her physical interest in him. Even in their heated moments she preferred clear direction and communication over theatrics. "What colony are you from?" he asked, relating more than he thought possible to her story.

"The name of my village is of no matter. I posed as the best conjurer in a place where smiths make a living selling weapons, armor, and gems. As the best mage in my vicinity, I received recognition on the world stage. When I arrived at Shadow Hills, I had to learn quickly, but need I bore you with that process? I'm certain you know what it is like to practice one craft and live another. You are a mage at heart, yes?"

Why did she sound so definite? Chills ran down his arms. He'd never considered himself a mage, just someone who enjoyed magickal crafts. To be labeled with such an official title by someone who spent her life around other mages made him confident in that hidden aspect of his life for the first time. If she believed he was a mage and still found him interesting, even attractive, then why hide his identity from the rest of the realm?

It's the mentors... They'd never let me compete as a male mage. I had to hide my abilities and practice sword-crafting.

"You see?" she asked. "This is why I value hope. Without it, I would have never taken the chance to study conjuration, despite finding my odds to be slim. I would've never taken the chance to send you a note. And why did you send one to me? I am no dark mentor, but perhaps, deep down, you envisioned a terrible future for yourself. You are finding a way, yes, and also taking a chance. Hope is all we have when all seems lost. It's what allows us to keep acting. I'm sure you had hope when first arriving in Shadow Hills. But this kingdom has made you comfortable. I see the potential in you, Aramis. You still sent me that letter. You believe you can change the fate of many fae in this realm... if only you had hope."

"But what if I fail?" Aramis asked. He didn't see the need to hide his fears and counterarguments when she could effortlessly unwind them. "It hurts so much more to fail when you have hope. With *action* alone, there is no emotional punishment—only two outcomes to every goal: successful and unsuccessful. Hoping for success grants nothing but suffering. It takes up space in the mind. Hope uses energy I could spend on planning—"

"Do you want to live your life avoiding suffering?" The female who'd simultaneously made his world more real than he could ever imagine, breathing life into his passion with words he wished to express, painting a perfect picture of his struggles and insecurities, also made him feel spineless.

He might not have thought about matters as much as he should have. Not only was his situation a shade less than common, but he spent most of his life complaining from a cynical perspective. Before seeing Simmia tonight, he'd practically given up on the tournament that tested males for their skills in male crafts. *There is no chance for me to win and become king...*

But he always wondered why the future queen had to be summoned from another realm. Why not host a tournament to test females in female skills? Better yet, why not have one big tournament to determine which two fae would make for the best-rounded king and queen?

"Suppose I agree with you," Simmia said. "Hope of a complete change in the Shadow Hills tournament might be too much to ask. One cannot expect a guild of male mages to form overnight. But do you think the future queen—the Asenath, as you say in this kingdom—do you think she will arrive this season?"

Aramis diverted his gaze. Was this the reason she invited him over? To try and prompt him into some further form of rebellion? It felt hard to be defensive while shirtless, so he finally pulled up the upper portion of his cloak. "Why do you ask?"

"Only..." Simmia seemed to choose her words carefully. "I see things a bit differently. For example, where is our current queen?"

The current queen of Shadow Hills had in fact been missing for weeks. It was no secret. Aramis discussed the matter with Garrett and Kollin almost daily. The lack of parties searching for the lost queen made them suspicious. The council completely neglected the disappearance of a key figure, proceeding with pre-tournament rituals as if nothing were wrong and everyone else should also forget.

But something about the air of Simmia—his challenger—made Aramis want to defend the council. What power could they maintain if they didn't work to preserve the image of the kingdom?

"If our current queen is not present, what makes you think we are ready to summon the Asenath?" She let the question permeate the room before speaking again. "It seems the council is already tipping the kingdom's balance in their own favor. You should also see it yourself. Do not lose your outsider's perspective."

Aramis didn't want to respond. If the council meant to hide the queen's disappearance, getting at the heart of what was wrong felt more important than being right and defending the kingdom. But a part of him struggled deeply with discrediting his old understanding of the kingdom, and how he'd silenced himself and all of his potential in hopes of succeeding.

How could the council lie so blatantly to the citizens?

That was the problem with hope. It made him believe falsehoods and allowed him to sit in ignorance. He became too trusting of the council above him, to the point where he'd fallen asleep and they'd shuffled the queen away without question.

Simmia was right about him, and how he'd hoped his entire life. It was impossible to act without hope. Only, he'd been hoping for the wrong thing. He felt an urge to defend the council, but why?

She said it herself:

He wanted to avoid suffering. For the longest time, he'd been *hoping* the council hadn't deceived him. He wanted to ignore the role he had to play in this kingdom, and here Simmia was, attempting to pull courage out of him. *Was* this *her plan?*

He tightened the loose belt around his cloak. "Where else do you think our kingdom is lacking? If you don't care to elaborate."

"They cannot hear us within these conjured walls." Simmia's calm and quick response angered him more. This probably meant the things she said were true. "So I will speak that which they would exile me for saying. Yet I ask: do you believe my words are true?"

The question caught Aramis off-guard, as did the way she peered at him with tear-shaped eyes from beside her raised shoulder, hands cupped together as she awaited his answer; eyes seducing like dark red orbs—pulling, wanting to consume him.

"Yes," he said, and he meant it.

"It seems rather backward to elect our king based on four petty games. Moreover, your females are experts in one dimension and entirely incompetent in others. Same with your males. Instead of everyone learning a few crafts here and there, joining guilds that interest them, you have a rigid structure that a training fae must follow, prescribed to them in adolescence when they have yet to change over and again. Do you expect fae to know their life path at the green age of fifty? Look into the past: Would you have correctly predicted your fate at such an age? Ask me then, and I would have said yes." Simmia laughed, placing a hand over her stomach. "And I couldn't have been more wrong."

Aramis took a deep breath. He found the moccasin for his left foot and searched for the other. "I used to think sword smithing was for me." If he had the opportunity to change, Aramis would've much rather joined the alchemy guild a few years into his training, where males practiced the art of magick under the guise of energy transfiguration.

Simmia's speech gained a pitch of excitement. "Shadow Hills assigns *one* task for each fae to master, based on nothing more than a birth signature. This is not the way to foster passion and great fae.

Whose destiny will ever be found in such a rigid template? Things must be allowed to change for growth to occur. We must be allowed to hope." Simmia shifted in the bed, covering her nakedness with the wool blanket. "And yet, the council seems to secretly hope against us."

As Aramis slipped on his second moccasin, Simmia sat upright on the edge of the bed. The way she moved—smooth and precise—gave Aramis reason to pause. He regretted having to leave. Over time, Aramis had come to question the tournament from many different angles, and Simmia made these doubts impossible to ignore. Come to find that there were others in the kingdom who wanted to explore crafts forbidden to them. It made him sad to know that so many out there struggled as he did—worse, if they could not sneak away and practice—but it also made him nervous to know that Simmia told him this for a reason. She believed he could make a change, and he almost didn't want the responsibility for those lives and their future. He was only trying to make his own life better.

So many questions ran through his mind. What was it like to spend life with a female, as if she were closer than a friend? His life would be dramatically different if he took this moment to ask Simmia if she would sneak out of the castle with him, escaping on a shipping float to some distant realm, maybe where she was from, where they'd spend thousands of years getting to know one another. That one decision would change his fate forever. He would be lying if he said it didn't pull him with the same attraction as Simmia's aura.

But that would mean living in fear. Aramis raised a maroon hood over his head.

Simmia stood and draped her arms over his shoulders, pressing her naked hips against his own. Her finger traced curled hairs along his chest. "I hope I will see you again."

"We have to wait for the tournament to end. I wouldn't want to tip the balance..." Repeating those words felt like admiring shackles on his wrist. He stared deep into her eyes. Throughout the night, he'd seen an inexplicable shimmer there. But now there was nothing.

"Good luck," she said.

His grip loosened, savoring the last touches of her soft skin, and trying to remember the curves of her waist. Aramis nodded. "Good luck to you." He searched for more to say but the only words he thought of sounded fake and overused. Soon enough, he descended, unseen, through the corridors of the female castle.

—

Twin moons in different shadowy phases dipped below the horizon far north. Dewy grass brushed against his ankles as Aramis trudged back through the garden, footprints behind him marking his strown path. With one last look up to Simmia's window, he left longing feelings behind as best as he could and exited from the trees, whose leaves curled in upon themselves, protecting a soft, inner barrier of illumination from its outer half of absorbent chlorophyll.

Contemplating Simmia's words, which seemed wiser by the moment, Aramis found that he could think of a hundred better ways to find a more fitting king than having a tournament. Allowing females to interact with males would be a start. Keeping fae entirely separated by gender in their developmental years did nothing but cause a severe divide when they expected the two groups to spend their lives together. And what was their reasoning: A lofty word called *balance*?

He finally reached the wide front doors of the male castle and ventured around the outer edge, returning to the back corridors. The outer portion of the castle grew out of a rocky ridge. After a few feet of solid ground, the ridge dropped off to many segmented clefts of sharp rock. Aramis retrieved the enchanted shield he'd hidden inside one of these nearby crevices.

He hopped into the curved portion of the shield with his legs crossed. It took a decent amount of force to push the lever and raise from the ground, and even more strength to keep the lever in place while hovering in front of his window, trying and failing to lift it open. A surge of panic rushed through him. He *knew* he'd left it unlocked. Beads of sweat trickled down the side of his face. There was only one reason why it would've been locked again.

He tried using the windowsill as leverage. He noticed a thin purple barrier lining the outer edges of where stone met stained glass. A rune bound the window shut, simple but effective, and it would stay shut against any counter-rune Aramis had ever learned.

Someone knew he'd been gone.

Panic spread throughout his body as sheer dread. The world went gray and cold despite the rising sun. His life seemed condensed down to this one fatal moment.

Nobody would want to be his mate after this incident. He'd be labeled as wild and insubordinate. For the rest of his life, Aramis would be alone without the opportunity to study the magick he loved. Already, the shield supporting his body drifted down; any remaining hope depleted. His future slipped away quicker than the castle's stones passing in front of him. The shield struck the ground with a *thump*.

"There he is! I told you! *Ha!*" The voice was ecstatic and unfortunately recognizable. *Brok*.

The smithing mentor, Sinisar, stood next to him in his customary red robe with his customary look of disgust. But there was more to the look this time around. As he stormed up to Aramis, hands balled into fists at his side, satisfied wrinkles appeared in the corners of his eyes, turning the look from disgust to smugness. "Let's see you use magick to try and get out of this one." He grabbed a tight hold of Aramis's wrist before looking back to the castle side, where they'd been hiding around the sharp corner. "Thank you, Brok. You may return to your study." Sinisar's face returned to patronize Aramis, plastered with disdain. "*Get up.*"

When Aramis stood with dignity, the mentor kicked away his modified shield. "And theft, *pfft*. I'll remember to notify the council." The hand clamping on his wrist made a vicious twist left, the world taking on a falling, spinning turn.

Aramis surrendered to the cobalt vortex of a portal, along with his fate.

❧ 6 ❧
COUNSEL

Aramis found his footing within a spacious, chilly room. Sinisar loosened the claw-like grip on his forearm with a grumble.

Half of the room's floor was patterned with off-white stone, burning in golden sunlight emanating from the far windows. The light crept up to the very edge of the square stones, cut off definitively by cold, dark wood, sturdy beneath his low-heeled flats. A sharp breeze brought goosebumps to his skin.

Twisting green vines climbed up where the floors met the walls, wrapping their way around sconces alight with berry-colored flames. That violet flame, a trick belonging to female fae alone, showed Aramis he was in the legendary quarters of the elder council, where all primary crafts were expressed through fanciful decor—the moving vines of elemental magick, bright sunlight of the divine, and dark magick's creaking wood and purple flames.

He should have felt fortunate to be in the presence of such grand symbolism. He should have been honored to have the time and attention of every mentor. But it wasn't the beneficial sort of attention.

Focusing on the ground, where stone and light ended, Aramis hid his face beneath his hood, glad to be in the darker side of the room. His young male face would've inspired nothing but resentment from the council toward the reckless fae, abusing the tools of magick for his own personal gain.

He risked a glance past the corner of his hood, following gem-lined pathways—slivers and cracks in the flooring filled with speckled rock—leading to monumental thrones made of stone or wood, depending upon their position in the hall. His curiosity quickly dimmed after meeting the disgusted face of a female council member—Vis, the elemental mentor, who embodied the very desires of the natural realm.

Rejected by the definition of grace.

Working up the bravery to raise his head a second time, he counted ten thrones spaced evenly around him, and eight mentors sitting in various postures of interest. Their mature wings extended in wide breadths, layered with vibrant colors and intricate patterns that made his lack of life experience with the crafts they signified so apparent. Every problem of the realm he'd pointed out with Simmia suddenly felt vague and underdeveloped in front of those who had seen so much more.

From the old stories, he recalled traditional customs specifying that four councilmembers sat on the female side of the elder's quarters, represented by a long strip of diamond rock running across the wall above their thrones. The stones also gleamed on both armrests of their royal seats, carved from the forest trees to signify the process of life, wisdom, and growth. On the other half of the room sat four male fae, indicated by the red stone of sumé on thrones of gray rock carved out of the reaching mountains—the eternal and divine. All councilmembers wore their most luxurious gowns, adorned with sashes and pointed caps to celebrate tournament week. Their stressed faces nullified the effect of any formality.

"Lock him up." Sinisar pulled himself into the room's second-to-last open seat. "Place him in our deepest dungeon, far below the mines. He deserves to rot in the darkness for tempting our kingdom with a fall. What do we lose, a weak male, unable to resist his basic desires? The benefits outweigh the costs, my king. These acts *spread*. They are as contagious as boiler pimples."

Is this a trial? The room's frigid air burrowed into Aramis' bones. He'd thought of so many consequences before sending his letter to

Simmia but when it came to the garden, he simply went. Both acts of sending notes and meeting with a female contestant broke the rule of abstinence, but not equally. Sleeping with Simmia felt more severe. Perhaps because it wasn't just one moment of weakness. He gave into temptation over and again...

Again, he was only curious. The urge to say as much came up but he wisely fought it away. They wouldn't want to hear about how he came to understand what being with a female fae was like, and how it might benefit him in the future—why did they try to act like the two fae weren't different? Why did the council despise the intensity of his interest, and their own? He'd seen how they suppressed their sexual appetite for one another when he spotted her across the banquet table, partially failing when the mead continued to flow. It was plain unfair to uphold odd restrictions when the councilmembers didn't adhere to their own ideals.

"I don't see any need for debate," Sinisar continued. "Our kingdom is in a state of... of..." It seemed to take a great effort for him to find the next word. "Development. Here is a clear opportunity to show our youth where we draw the line. Honestly, do you see this type of disobedience benefitting us one, two hundred years down the way?" The armory mentor crossed his arms, long nose lifted into the air. "You told me to bring the young male before you. I am awaiting his consequences."

"Hmm," the low grunt came from the king's throne directly across the room, where the light shone heavily. "I should've known this was the one who broke tradition. Forgive me, Sinisar, my professional in the art of smithing, but you're always quick to find the negative. It's no fault of your own. It even benefits your craft. When making weapons with a minimalist mindset, things don't go wrong nearly as much, and our kingdom doesn't end up spending frivolously. You find the errors, the weak points, if you will, and remove them without consideration. But do you ever ask yourself: what's the utility of a rejected soul?"

Sinisar's lips curled. "Not when the reputation of my kingdom is on the line, dear king. I find it much better to act in the present and think later."

The king spoke deliberately, surveying the room as if accustomed to the bickering and the vines and the dancing violet flames. "You are but one member on this council, in this kingdom. One opinion." The tip of his pointed crown held a circular gray stone, as transparent as a diamond if it weren't for the infrequent yellowed streaks. "Does anyone else see the need for debate? Must we discuss hiding this occurrence from the rest of the realm, or what might be done with the female in question? I believe the answer is yes. If anything, we may claim to have given the youth a fair trial."

Fae mentors murmured their agreements.

"*I* am a member of this council," Sinisar belted. "This young fae used his skills in magick to obtain sexual relations within the female quarters. What more needs to be said?" Those last words echoed in the open space between walls of vine. Sinisar waved to the diamond-half of the room. "While we are on the topic, you should punish your female with equal severity. As far as I'm concerned she was a temptress. I saw her wearing those flimsy foreign dresses, hardly reaching past her waist. I know what she was trying to do."

"Our students are our concern," said a member of the council under diamond rock. Her voice sounded like one would think coming from the mentor of divine light—full of life. A gown of gold silk dripped over her body, accenting her green eyes, which cast a spell on Aramis; they seemed friendly, the only friendly eyes in the room. The rest of her features were amber like her skin—almost burned—seeming to glow with their own inner sunlight waiting to burst forth. A set of wings behind her shone so faint a pale yellow that he questioned their existence. Her words didn't travel through petty air to reach to his ears, either—but through light. They arrived faint and distant to him in the shade yet still maintained their musical quality. "This issue revolves around the male in question. His premature mate is from another kingdom, operating under different beliefs. She has little to do with this case."

"She seduced our young fae," Sinisar shouted, his voice like iron striking iron. "Surely you're bright enough to see the need for conse-quences."

Lucilia, head member of the female council, watched the male mentor's composure rise and fall, words bunching together on the edge of his lips. Once the echoes of Sinisar's voice quieted and his dribbling ended, she held every drop of the room's attention. "And this will likely keep happening if there is no change in your castle, my dear smithing mentor. It is my understanding that male warriors are expected to withstand any form of temptation. This is why kingdoms across the realm purchase our armies. Yet, your male failed the part... and it does not appear to be his first failure."

While Sinisar chewed his lip, the center fae directed the gray gem in his crown toward Aramis. In the prime of his days, he spoke in slow, intimidating deliverances. "Do you deny these allegations?"

"No," Aramis managed to say, briefly longing for the future he might have had if he'd chosen to escape with Simmia. "I cannot deny anything... but—"

"So you stepped foot in the female castle?"

Unable to vocalize the truth, Aramis nodded.

Council members shuddered at the broken law. They threw whispers across the room in the form of colorful wisps.

"It would be foolish to lock this contestant in a dungeon, leaving it to the kingdom to spread stories about his escapade." The king spoke aloud for the first time in what felt like years.

"What are you saying?" Sinisar begged. "He's broken the kingdom's law. He must see the lowest of lows for his misdeeds, where burglars, thieves, and every other law-breaking fae—"

"Answer this question," interrupted the king. "How will other kingdoms react when they hear of an insubordinate young fae who had his fun in Shadow Hills?"

A long silence followed. It was difficult to tell whether the question was rhetorical, because it was difficult to read the king. "You cannot answer? I figured," the king chuckled. "Our warriors will be the laughingstock of the realm. Other kingdoms will know of our inability to find an Asenath this coming season."

"Don't we have enough to hide?" asked Lucilia, the divine mentor of light. "Perhaps knowledge of this misdeed and its accompanying punishment will strengthen our men. Call them to a higher purpose."

The king scoffed. "You of all people should know the risk of rumors traveling the realm like trade caravans. Secrets breed resentment and anger, which lead to war."

The divine mentor bowed her head and nodded. Already the council descended into their petty politics, and Aramis took note of the divine mentor's apparent feelings of inadequacy, and how she was so eager to do away with him. Even those who practiced magick wouldn't accept him because he was a male, and traditionally, such crafts were reserved to the female castle, less the balance of the realm be thrown off.

The king delivered his point with his hands gesturing proudly. "If this rumor of our insubordinate young fae spread about, powerful armies would descend upon our weak territory within the coming tournament days, like crows to a carcass. We all know it is only illusion keeping us safe from the realm's greater, older powers. Let us be truthful. And when our crafted armies seem weak, that forest becomes a bridge with enough food and cover to transport an army, and our untrained youth will be forced to fight an invasion. We will be no match. Other kingdoms will form alliances against us, no matter how they disperse our wealth. Young and old fae will watch their mates die, and then lie next to them."

A mentor seated under the side of red sumé stood, wings dark and wide. His growing presence seemed to consume a portion of the room's sunlight. "May I suggest a punishment that does not involve underground prison cells, or war between kingdoms?" When no one spoke, he continued, directing his words to Sinisar and the divine mentor. "In my proposition, this male before you will be adequately punished, suffering more than he would within the deepest, darkest dungeons of Losamara."

The council exchanged glances. Aramis felt as if he were in some odd torture chamber where the mentors bounced around ideas about what would make him suffer the most. He just wanted the undefined severity of his punishment to end.

"I believe everyone is at least willing to listen," said the king.

Sinisar scoffed, but the mentor with an alternate suggestion was Morian, the council fae most skilled in alchemy. His control over the transmutation of matter made him one of the more respected mentors.

Morian's field of study was a venture from which few fae returned, often losing themselves in the temptation of resurrecting the dead—typically a loved one—creating stereotypes about alchemists as a whole, which for some reason, they embraced.

"I propose assigning a task for our young fae to make right the crime he committed against our kingdom," Morian said. "Let us open our minds. As our king mentioned, we must innovate, be clever in our concealment of this egregious error. Shadow Hills is already near the brink of dissolution..." He gestured toward the last empty throne at the far end of the room, but none of the councilmembers looked. They knew he spoke of the absent queen, who had disappeared three weeks ago. Like Aramis and his friends and other fae in his guild, none of the councilmembers directly mentioned the queen's disappearance, preferring to hint at the fact with passive language.

"Let us not forget who we have before us," Morian continued. "Does anyone here know our young fae well enough to recall his name?" Everyone hung on the thread of silence, wondering where it led. "His name is Aramis. According to our criteria for male fae, this contestant is below average as a smith, and anything else for that matter. But when you witness his inclination for the study of magick..."

"*Pshh*," the sound seemed to escape from Sinisar.

A few wisps made their way from the female side of the room to the male. Morian paid them no mind.

"Perhaps this fae's skill with magick can help us locate our new Asenath, reading the faults in this season's compass. We might benefit from the perspective of a male competitor. Someone who will be in the tournament themself." Mumbles of disagreement arose, which Morian quelled without allowing them a moment to fester. "Let us try this method. If he successfully fixes thee compass and navigates to the realm of the Asenath, his punishment will be to retrieve the future queen."

So, this season's Asenath is missing too? The fae who would become queen—beside whom all of the males would compete to rule—had yet to be summoned, and the tournament would begin in a few days.

"Perhaps I heard you wrong," said Vis, the elemental mentor. She wore a leaf-covered headdress decorated with fruits of the land. A pearlescent glitter showed off exposed olive skin—very much of it— covered by the occasional twisting vine. Aramis blushed at the shine of her olive skin, and tried to keep his gaze elsewhere. "Do you suggest having this inexperienced fae fiddle with our precious compass portal?"

"None of the female mentors have been able to fix it, and we must find our future queen soon enough. Please, don't underestimate his experience with the art of magick. Is your memory so short?" Morian considered the rest of the room with a lifted brow. "Just this evening, he'd been able to sneak past every one of us and enter the female castle. I suspect that wasn't his first time, either."

After a short consultation on the side of diamond stone, the mentor of flora and fauna spoke again. "Even if the portal is fixed by his hand, you suggest punishing our young fae by having him meet the future queen? Would this not be a lovely moment for the male contestant, bonding him with the Asenath on an intimate level? He would be the first fae she sees. She will see him as her savior. Or captor. Whichever the portal deems more alluring."

"Would such a short meeting bond the two souls?" asked the male mentor nearest to Aramis, famed for his skills in the craft of architecture.

"It is an interesting route for punishment," said Morian. "And yes, difficult for the ignorant mind to comprehend." He sat back on his throne, eyes searching through empty air as if balancing a complex alchemical equation in his head. "His soul would be bonded with the Asenath if he is the one who summons her. We always rinse the new queen and her summoner of any lingering bonds... I suggest we avoid doing so with Aramis. The criminal will help retrieve the Asenath, and as a result, he will yearn for her all his life, never to be loved in return. This is his punishment."

A few council members nodded, sending wisps through the air. Most remained silent.

"One-way binding," pondered another female fae—Celeste. Beads of chestnut wood on her clothing matched the color of her wings. Metal rings lined one nostril and both of her ears, jingling as she moved her head. "I understand. And you're aware that a lack of skill with the compass portal could bring one to an unknown, uninhabitable realm?"

"I am aware," Morian said. "And there he will find nothing but toxins and death."

"What of the other kingdoms?" asked Celeste. "Your plan doesn't heal the bleeding wound of gossip."

Morian jumped at the question. "That's just it—Aramis will compete in the tournament." Fae around the room made eye-contact with one another but never opened their mouths. "He was never gifted in the male crafts. I foresee him losing every tournament game... Don't you?"

While the insult burned, Aramis was grateful for this new form of punishment, which was far better than wasting away in the underground mines. He had never really been in love, and therefore, he had no idea what it felt like not to be loved in return, but it was certainly better than the stench of the dungeon's rot.

"So be it," said the divine mentor of light. "We will send the foreign student back to her homeland, serving as a lesson for future recruits. Let her spill a story about losing everything at the hand of a male."

"But she did nothing," Aramis said before he could bite his tongue.

The council ignored the statement, if they even heard it to begin with.

Simmia... The one who had risked everything to show him a new outlook toward the kingdom, encouraging him to embrace the side of him that the kingdom oppressed. *I'm so sorry.*

One day, he vowed to visit her village, to find it somehow, and make it up to her if he could.

But she would want to kill him if they ever saw each other again. He couldn't blame her. Everything she risked to get close to the mine reserves of Shadow Hills—the lies and deceit, living life doing work she hated just for the occasional gem—and he was careless enough to throw it all away. *Perhaps I should stay out of her life.*

The king leaned forward, steepled fingers held at his lips. The throne next to him remained desolate. "We will task Aramis with retrieving the future queen, testing his skills in dark conjuration. If the compass portal is mended, a servant imp will accompany his venture to the future queen's realm, ensuring her arrival. Then, the future queen's bond will be erased, while his own will remain. Aramis will then compete in the tournament and inevitably fail. His punishment for such liberal desire is unrequited love. Objections?"

No one released a wisp.

The king rose, translucent wings spreading far, brown and beige veins pulsing throughout. "So it is settled. Throw him in the mines until the morrow."

7

IMPISH BEHAVIOR

In a small mine cart bumping along an underground track, Aramis zoomed past walls filled with black soot, barren of gems. The upper portions of the mine were sourced long ago during the days when Samara, the founding mentor of dark magick, walked in freshly carved corridors.

Sinisar the smithing mentor piloted the small cart. He frequently slammed on squealing brakes, shouting at workers on the upcoming track, making them dodge aside at the last moment.

The two kept traveling deeper into the mines.

Neither spoke.

Why couldn't Morian have escorted me? They could've talked about fixing the compass portal, which provided the slight chance Aramis had of survival. He could either correctly locate the Asenath, or travel to some unknown realm, likely deadly. He needed hints or advice, anything to improve his chances of summoning the queen. After receiving a few murderous glances, he figured Sinisar wouldn't let him out of his sight until his idea of a proper punishment was carried out.

The world deep below the grass gained a dream-like essence the further they ventured—tilted, winding, and uncertain in the violet light cast by the sconces overhead.

He questioned whether he genuinely had good intentions regarding Simmia. Was he risking his friendship and a chance, though slim, at becoming king, supposedly throwing off the balance of the kingdom? And for what? Aramis acted under the belief that he was just curious and never saw a need to hide his curiosity—until it got the best of him.

Had he been chasing desire he was too weak to ignore, driven by forces he was too distracted to sense, like the female councilmember said? With more thought, it became easier to see how he might have been breaking rules too complex for his understanding, tempting a dormant monster he couldn't contend with. Maybe he ignored the repercussions of such a rule because it sounded so meaningless—*do not pursue that which you desire.*

Now he revealed the kingdom's true underbelly and its missing queen.

Even in the vibrating, screeching cart, he longed to turn back time using some strand of dark magick and have that letter in his hands, this time being more careful with Brok. The only thing he regretted was the fact that Simmia had to leave Shadow Hills and her studies. She had risked everything, they both had, but somehow her purpose seemed purer, mentioning the flaws of the kingdom with the intention of correcting them.

Memories of her soft skin, and her long eyelashes fluttering up at him under thick ruby hair, burned in his chest. He missed how she would lie on her side and tilt her head while asking a question, as if truly wanting to hear his answer, whatever it may have been.

The dark mine with its less frequent distractions seemed to encourage these torturous thoughts and intensify his guilt.

Their cart came to a grinding stop. Refusing to look his way, the mentor opened the cart door and climbed up to a chest-high platform, hardly wide enough to fit them both. He fumbled through a set of keys, gripping one and holding it out to Aramis. The number three was carved with precision into its side. The smithing mentor sneered down at Aramis. "Think you're not going in?" He stuck a thumb toward a nearby set of vertical bars, and behind them, a wide rocky cell.

Empty, dark space.

Aramis joined the mentor on the cramped ledge, his elbow brushing against light armor.

"Are you aware what type of lock this is?" Sinisar asked, pointing to a hefty lock secured around a thicker chain, stretched across the segmented bars.

Aramis failed to attend Sinisar's lectures more than any other class, though not out of spite. Armory lessons were in the morning, and Aramis practiced magick late into the night hours, when he could. Waking up after an hour of rest to go and sweat, blister, and heat ore rarely seemed appealing.

"No."

"Good. If you don't understand how it works, you can't use your prissy little tricks to break out." Sinisar plunged the key into the lock, opened the gate, and clutched Aramis's collar. "And I know you'd try."

The young fae's blood heated, mind and morals growing fuzzy with anger. He wanted to lash out, throwing Sinisar into the mine tracks where some cart would hopefully run him over.

But this was a mentor, the smithing mentor most skilled in fighting with weapons, and he likely carried a push dagger on him now. He became conscious of Sinisar's expanded wings, tinted with glowing veins of red. Searing hot, they pulsed with a fiery, furnace-like glow.

Had Aramis been in an actual fight, he'd conjure a ghostly-looking dagger—if he could focus enough—and extend the blade until it sank into the mentor's gut.

"You're not going to throw off the balance of this kingdom." Sinisar growled. "I won't let it happen. Our males are weak, and it is fae like you who are to blame. You wretched, inconsiderate waste of a male. Making others think it is fine to disregard the longest-living rules of our time. Those principles have maintained the wealth of our kingdom and allowed it to thrive. Truthfully, I don't know why they are letting you live."

A force—too strong to have come from another fae—launched Aramis into the cell. He barely caught his footing when he turned back and shouted, "I'm not the one who is weak."

But Sinisar had already secured the lock and was climbing back into the mine cart.

In that cell, it felt like the darkness pressed upon him, wrapping its tendrils around his throat and tightening, suffocating.

Aramis doubted he'd ever see daylight again.

—

Sometimes, there is only a distant ray of bright, sunny, golden light that fae can use to guide themselves from one point to the next—a north star of sorts. When fae look into this divine light, they see the best version of themselves, and strive to climb out of darkness and attain.

Other times, dimmer, violet light provokes fae just as effectively. This odd, ethereal substance isn't so much seen as it is felt—moving through walls and stone and books and instruments for ages—and a sudden urge overcomes the whole body, launching fae into passionate movement before they can think. Fae typically run from the violet light, as opposed to chasing the golden rays, because unlike the divine, a dimmer, purple glow evokes pain.

Both are forms of light, each speaking at different volumes to different fae. Both can be mastered. And the presence of both dark and divine is required in any healthy kingdom.

—

It wasn't the bars on the dungeon cell that kept Aramis miserable, but the utter darkness between carts. Aramis spotted the passing mine carts a mile down the tunnel because of the front lantern's dim orange, swinging glow. He counted three so far and looked out for more.

He studied the distant glow of cart lamplights, shining brighter as the carts approached, giving him something to think about besides the torture of his mistake. Then the mine cart squealed by, its driver typically wearing some sort of head-wrap, and the putrid scent of rotting rat carcasses would waft through the cell's open face. Aramis had come to appreciate the change in smell after the first two carts. It was better than growing used to the scent.

Eventually, his chin bobbed down to his chest. The jagged rock pressing into his back hurt less and less. He didn't want to rest down here. It didn't feel safe. But considering he'd been up for so long, he no longer had the energy to support the weight of his eyelids.

He awoke to tiny, particularly weak hands vigorously shaking his knee. "Wake up, wake up, wake up," urged a sniveling voice. "We don't have long."

Aramis scrambled to his feet. A waist-high, pot-bellied figure crouched before him with a waving tail and thin wings. It glowed like a bright red gem, fluttering back, but not far enough.

Shocked into action, Aramis kicked the creature with the speed of a decent swordsman, his foot connecting with its gut.

The tiny thing cried *oof* as it flew back.

While the red creature shivered there against the wall, using its thin arms to recover and stand to its feet, Aramis had time to study: it had clawed feet—three talons on each—and was surrounded by a reddish hue. Little red, curly hair covered its body everywhere except for its wide red eyes and two white horns, which protruded in different curving directions out of its head. The creature wore only a silk loincloth.

"Imp?"

Occasionally, imps were called upon for dirty, quick deeds. Their generational knowledge about conjuration magick made deception easy for the creatures, what with them darting anywhere they pleased and the ability to render themselves invisible. Aramis needed to show confidence and strength in case Sinisar sent this imp to murder him.

The imp struck its hairy chest. "*Hack. Haacggk. H-auuggghck.*" It stood straight, barely reaching up to Aramis's waist. "I'd prefer if you call me Erlick, you fae contestant. How would you like it if I called you by your particular species, as if it's all I see? Fae, fae, fae, so arrogant in his way, he'll *KICK AN IMP ACROSS THE ROOM!*"

"*Shh.*" Aramis glanced out at the barred darkness. "How did you get in here?" He asked the question with a stern, hopefully intimidating voice.

Erlick groaned disapprovingly. "No apologies. Straight to the questions. I thought I was dealing with a fae that had sense... I'm beginning to doubt myself." Erlick brushed himself off and crossed his arms.

Despite his puny stature, his face drooped in several areas—unsatisfied and aged.

After hearing the imp's tone, Aramis should've felt less threatened. But what the creature could do with magick remained to be seen.

"What I'm *doing here* is trying to help you," Erlick said.

Aramis studied the imp's stern expression—tail moving solemnly behind it, spearheaded at the end. "Why would you want to help me? Unless you can find the Asenath, I need you to leave. I need to focus."

"Yea... An awful lot of focusing you were doing."

Aramis had no idea how long his eyes had been closed before the imp's appearance. Had he fallen asleep? "Answer my question, if we have so little time."

A proud shimmer appeared in the imp's platelike eyes.

"You know how to fix the compass portal?" Aramis asked. "You have to tell me."

Erlick trembled with sourness. "Have to? No, I don't. I absolutely don't have to do anything—way too eager, young fae. You're way too ready to jump. I can see we're not too skilled in the art of bartering. Are you that excited to fall in love with someone who will never love you in return?"

"I'm excited to escape this cell," Aramis said. "To live with some sense of a normal life. I don't need love as long as I can live."

The imp's face remained unfazed, as if he didn't believe a word Aramis said. "You're not entirely unreasonable... Just naive. I suppose I will tell your desperate soul that I do know how to fix the portal. I am an imp, as you were so quick to point out. And now that I've finally gotten you in the right position, I..." The imp paused, hairy eyelids widening while his tiny hand covered thin lips. He knocked himself in the head over and over with an open palm. "Curse me and my hellish mouth thrice."

Aramis stomped toward the imp. "Got me in the right position?" Tired of asking questions, he stared down at the creature. He might be unable to take the imp in a duel of magick, but if he could prove to the council that this imp forced him into this situation, he might be freed. "You made me fall for Simmia?"

"That was all you and your dirty mage mind. And I thought you didn't care about love?"

Aramis fumed. "Then you're the one who told the council about Simmia. About me."

"Technically, no. I didn't tell them anything. I only woke up Brok and led him to your room. The council doesn't know I exist just yet. I mean, they haven't summoned me to help you yet. Not until you find the Asenath. You see? It's all a part of my intricate plan." The imp's air of confidence faded when he opened his oval eyes. "But, I-I mean, you were the one who did all the escaping and rune-breaking, and might I say you were rather skilled in—"

Aramis sunk his face into his own cupped hands, sliding back down the wall in hopes that the agony of scraping rock would be enough to take away his mental anguish. "An imp... tricked me. An *imp*! A devious, good-for-nothing imp."

"Fine," Erlick said. "Did I alert that fuming armory mentor of your escape? Yes. Only because I have a greater plan. You're going to be a hero, Aramis."

"A hero?" he asked, dropping his hands to see if the imp was telling an awful joke. "Like in bedtime stories? Fighting dragons of the past?" The next words were hard to say, but he felt he had to say them out loud, admitting them to himself. "I've lost my chance at winning the tournament and making any real change. And this kingdom doesn't want a hero, anyway. Like you said, we're too stuck in our ways."

"As I recall, the council didn't change anything about the tournament to keep you from winning. They just assumed you lacked skill in the male arts."

The imp paused, but Aramis refused to look in his direction. He wasn't interested if there wasn't talk about fixing the portal.

"I'm sorry..." The imp actually managed to sound sincere. "Tell me why you wanted to compete with the other pea-headed contestants in this year's tournament? Why not run off and practice magick alone? You'd make for a decent warlock."

"The thought of living that secluded life terrifies me. I'd go insane."

As Aramis continued thinking, it seemed that secluded life was only half the issue with escaping from Shadow Hills. He really did want to love another fae, but it never seemed possible while practicing magick. He always thought he had to choose between being a decent, law-abiding male with a happy family, or a warlock who gave himself to a craft he'd never master.

"Most warlocks do," Erlick agreed.

Aramis hated how the imp acted like they were friends. He walked up to the bars of his cell and tried giving them a tug, but his fingers met an invisible barrier created when Sinisar fastened his special lock.

"How long have you been spying on me?" He asked the imp.

"Not necessarily spying. I've only been doing my job."

"I don't like the way you reword things. And following me around, watching everything I do, seems like an odd job. But let's say you're truthful, for now. Who hired you? I want to know how much they're paying. Tell me the value of my life."

"My job isn't to kill you. You'd be long gone by now. Dead and away. Fading mist in the light of these sconces. Nothing but a thought and—"

"Okay, I get it. Then, what is your job?"

"My job is to keep my job. Who do you think tends to the arenas for your games—provides concessions, flowers, and merchandise for the fans? Your tournament is a primary source of income for my agency."

"Agency?"

"Imp services," he said, touching the top of one curved horn as he bowed. "Our kind learns very quickly. The magick helps. When it comes time for the tournament, and your little council comes asking for help because the deepest darkness knows you fae wouldn't be able to coordinate a working ecosystem of shops and entertainment yourselves, what with all your internal politics and differing opinions on how things should be done. That's why your mentors want to change things—they disagree too often, and never step forward. One of your smarter mentors realized long ago, probably a mage of a sort, that we imps throw a tournament better than any of you fae. And when I receive your inter-realm message from your pretend-pious council, I know I will be able to travel with my family that season."

Aramis snorted. "You're helping me so you can get a vacation?"

"Amongst other things, I guess I'm upholding a lifestyle—fulfilling a desire for new things. Really, you're the one who should be worried. I could always bring my services to another realm. But what work could a fae find in an imp realm? None at all. This place is all you know. Fae society is very one-dimensional."

He snorted. "Step back and look at what would happen if the tournament didn't occur this season," Erlick said. "There would be no new king and queen and no new members on the council. Sounds beneficial for a select few, yea? Maybe those most eager to witness your demise?"

"The councilmembers..." The argument seemed futile, but Aramis realized he couldn't find a way to prove the imp wrong. Mentors planning to keep their positions on the council mirrored what Simmia was saying about the kingdom's innate corruption. Every action the council took made sense under the guise of their need to stay in power. They didn't want him to compete in the tournament because if he won, he would change the operations of the kingdom. Many would no longer have a say in which fae could practice which craft.

"The queen," he thought aloud. "Do you know why she disappeared?"

"Eh, yea. But it's sad. We have to be careful about how many sad stories we tell."

Aramis couldn't stop thinking about what it'd be like if the council never changed, the kingdom stuck in its ways forever. How many fae would be subjected to the same miserable existence he, Simmia, and an uncountable number of Tabula Rasa had to endure?

A slow shake of the head, and the imp's expression turned into a grin of pointed teeth as jagged as the Divine Mountains. "That's why the elders are so scared of you, my frightening fae. Why you were always on my radar." The imp shrugged, studying his cuticles. "Having you in the tournament is a real danger, given the types of games this year. I've seen what the games are testing for, put my greasy imp hands all over the schematics, and it's not the strongest fae this kingdom needs. We will all see as much when the portal opens for you. Only thing we need to do is get you to survive long enough to summon the Asenath."

Things were happening much too quickly for Aramis to comprehend, but that last bit about the Asenath made him even more worried. "That doesn't explain why you exposed me to the council," he said. "You could've let me be." He was about to say he was just fine on his own, but that wasn't true. "I would have been able to compete in the tournament myself. I might have won if the games were different like you claim. Then everyone could practice magick. Or whatever craft they choose."

"Eh, you never would've made it on your own, and you know this. You're a promising mage," Erlick said, snapping his fingers as if casting a spell from his hand. "We just need to get it out of you. You need what fae alchemists call a catalyst."

This time it was Aramis's turn to laugh. "I don't think you understand my punishment. They forbade from winning the tournament. Actually, they said they'd assign your kind to make sure..."

Now Aramis fully comprehended the imp's strategic planning skills, though he would never admit as much out loud. "So you're saying the tournament wasn't going to happen before? But it is now?"

"My two horns, this can't be the best your castle has to offer. What do you think is the result of the compass portal not functioning? No chance to summon the Asenath."

"Were you there during my trial?" Aramis made a concerted effort to ignore the chide. He couldn't remember seeing a barely clothed horned creature with a tail in that vast council room, though it was a distracting time and place.

"I'm everywhere. Even with you and your not-so-mate." The imp winked, rocking his tiny hips back and forth.

And he said fae are arrogant. Aramis couldn't let the creature go on, reaching out for Erlick's neck as the imp giggled—but before he could clutch the tiny pipe, the creature disappeared. His hand grasped thin air.

Aramis straightened and looked around the room.

Erlick was behind him. "Need direction?"

"How did you—"

"Go poof? Invisible?" He strutted forward again. "I'm an imp, a creature of the magick you study. Conjuration, to be exact. It's in my veins. I've lived secrets you could only wish to discover." Eyes closed, he spoke proudly with one finger raised in the air. "Such as how to fix the compass portal. You can buy the complete course for the infinitesimal price of 99 realm jumpers. I'll also take any of your fae currency if you happen to have some. It doesn't seem like you do."

Aramis considered yelling at the being to force out the information, but he had a feeling that wouldn't work. The imp would call him impatient and unmannered. Erlick wanted to do nothing but sit and talk about the concept, so he had to comply.

"Can you teach me then?" he asked. "I can't stay down here forever. You said we don't have much time."

"That's what I was looking for," Erlick said smugly. "Let me say your perseverance is what makes you different. That's why you study magick. Why you'll save the realm from its misbalanced forces. Why—"

"Please?" Aramis begged. "All I want is to know how to summon the future queen."

"Yes. Yea. *OK*. But I have to ask, how deep is your study?"

"What?"

"Magick, what else? The art of the soul and mind. Connection with nature and spirit. It's the energetic force that fills you with wonder and inspiration. The very essence of every creation, good or bad and everything in between. How deep does it run in your veins?"

Aramis thought hard about his answer. He didn't want to embarrass himself in front of someone so well-versed. "I've read about most forms of the craft except for dark and conjuration magick." He spoke confidently, though defending that statement might reveal a different story. "Those texts have been difficult to get my hands on."

"Yet those are the skills you'll need most." The imp gave a dismissive wave of his three-fingered hand. "Doesn't matter. Your knowledge of the divine and natural magicks will serve just fine. I can explain everything as long as you understand the fundamentals of the practice itself."

"Try me." Aramis crossed his arms in preparation.

The imp cleared its throat with another pounding fist to the chest. "Dark magick is energy fueled by emotion and intention, like any other magick. The difference is in the type of emotions various magicks deal with, yea? Here, we speak of the monumental factors capable of summoning darkness. Love and loathing, judgment and joy. Am I getting off track? Let me know."

"You're making sense." Actually, this was all Aramis ever wanted to understand. He just wanted the imp to continue. He'd never known of such intricacies within the dark magicks, or how certain emotions belong to light magick, such as joy and love had a place within the dark.

The imp shuffled closer, his hunched stature growing even more paranoid and secretive. He spoke in a whisper. "Do not be so fervent, young fae. That is precisely the wrong approach. Dark magick wipes out whole realms if a mage is not careful. Cosmic energies have that sort of power. We need someone brave enough to confront and tame these dark forces when the time comes, transmuting them into beneficial tools, lest the mentors drive us all to oblivion. Yea. *Oblivion.* You have the strength to do such things. You're in the right position." Another sly wink. "Now, thinking logically, what would make you fall in love with another being irrevocably, without condition, past your wildest imagination?"

Aramis felt a sensitive playfulness rising in his chest as he considered the question. He allowed his mind to wander, finding unpredictable thoughts.

He thought of Simmia, the beautifully high structure of her cheekbones, eyes of firelight staring back at him. The perfect movements of her toned, tight body...

But that didn't fulfill half of what Aramis envisioned when he imagined the qualities of a queen—someone he was supposed to love forever.

Nervous, he didn't know if he agreed with every definition he'd heard about beauty, let alone love—an emotion that seemed as foreign as distant kingdoms. He thought of old poets and how they described love as fleeting, how everything in the world faded except for the sweet taste of a partner's lips. Or like flowers, requiring a constant return of protection and care if they were to bloom. Occasionally, there was the contradictory mention of a tugging force of hostility, wherein one fae denied thoughts of another to the point where they became impossible to ignore. Once fed, those invasive feelings turned into undying appreciation.

The imp snapped his three fingers, producing a flat sound. "Hey, hey. Don't think of everything now. You have to keep it fresh, for when you get in front of the compass portal, or it won't work."

"Why?" Aramis asked.

"Same as every other conjuration spell. If you're thinking about some abstract version of the necessary object, you're not summoning the real thing. It's a false feeling, created for a specific purpose, and the magick turns false too. Your intentions aren't pure. You must focus on the real deal if you want to conjure. For instance, if you try to think back to this moment, or any other concept of a queen you might have conceived beforehand, the portal won't open to the rightful realm of your vision."

"But if I imagine the same concepts, isn't it all the same feeling? I'm fostering hope for love and using emotion to power the compass portal, funneled through my intention of finding the Asenath. If the thought is from the past, but I'm having the feeling now, why does it make a difference?"

"Yea... These are the intricacies of dark magick that make a mage good or great. Who said feelings couldn't be remembered, and sought after once again? This is a common path on which many-a-mage become lost. Not us imps. We know that old emotions are to be left in the past. We're entirely reasonable."

The words seemed to ring out in the cave as the imp's pupils darted to the side of Aramis. One of its thin, pointed ears turned. "Someone is coming. For you."

Aramis allowed himself a moment of panic before thinking clearly. "Is there anything else I should know?"

"A lot," Erlick said. "Too much. You hardly know a thing. But if I don't see you before you see the compass portal, think about the qualities of a queen you might seek. Things only you could know. Aspects that the council would never consider. But not now. Not until you reach the portal."

That wicked smile appeared again on the imp's face. Nevertheless, Aramis found he trusted the creature more than anyone on the council

—except maybe Morian, who had saved him from the suggested punishment of death.

Outside the cell, lantern light shone brighter from down the tunnel. The harsh glow was different than that of the other carts—bright yellow, chasing shadows into corners of his cell as brakes screeched and whined against the rails.

Turning back toward the shrinking darkness, Aramis found the imp had disappeared.

8

DIVINATION

When it came to imps, Aramis knew little more than what his "borrowed" conjuration texts mentioned about the creatures. In theory, imps were small, mischievous beings, often summoned for menial house tasks in exchange for fae metal and gems, which served across many realms as precious currency.

A few questionable tales and old song lyrics suggested the occasional imp as a mercenary or beneficent figure in fae history. But until his recent interaction, it never occurred to Aramis how integral the creatures were to their society, especially if they could listen in on every interaction without their presence being known. Erlick spoke as if he knew what happened between the council members of seven seasons ago.

In other words, he was a meddler like every other imp.

But Aramis couldn't dismiss the imp or anything he said. Erlick recalled his trial in front of the council with complete accuracy. The imp pointed out the fact that the current queen was missing while the council refused to acknowledge the idea of her.

He'd also recognized Aramis's natural inclination for magick, more than Garrett and Kollin ever had. Whenever Aramis cast a spell around his friends, they couldn't help but divert their eyes and move on to the next subject. They completely disregarded his magical abilities, so he stopped mentioning them.

Erlick made Aramis's desire to learn about magick seem normal, giving him hope when it came to fixing the portal and finding the Asenath. Sure, he might have snitched on Aramis for his own personal gain, but that didn't seem like anything new in the kingdom, and Aramis would much rather work with someone who wanted to spread the knowledge of magick and not keep it for themselves, like the council.

I can trust Erlick more than any of the elder fae.

The metallic screech of an approaching minecart called him back from thought—no, the sound had been Sinisar's mocking voice.

"… an alchemist and their loose tongue to ruin it for everyone. How long must we keep up this facade of ignorance? The king has been nothing but a procrastinating coward when it comes to granting your wishes. The youth is disobedient and directionless. We need a leader who takes change by the horns. A mentor who demands stability and authority in this kingdom."

Aramis gulped. Why had Sinisar come back so soon?

"All this time on the council, and you still haven't noticed?" A softer voice echoed from down the mine tunnel—words dancing through the air like soft rays of morning light. Music from some better place. "Dearest mentor, some believe the truth, while others invent it. The king is the face of our kingdom, but he answers to me." The grinding brakes of the mine cart grew louder, nearer. "We must maintain every false hope that the Asenath will be found. Many are quick to search for lies in the council's speech."

"Lies… *Hmph*. If only this were all as simple as lying."

"It is difficult," said the lighter voice. "Change must seem necessary if we expect the kingdom to follow. This means planting disdain for the current state of our kingdom into the minds of our people. Less like change, I think it should feel. More like adaptation toward a better way of living. An obvious improvement. The same way one might think of cleaning their residence, or drinking a potion to cure their illness."

Sinisar trod lightly on each word. "Of course, Lucilia. If fae expect change but feel powerless, who will our kingdom's residents confide in? They'll seek refuge with the council. What power will they have if they aim to revolt? I suppose, they could form an alliance amongst themselves..."

Aramis wouldn't have understood the conversation if Erlick hadn't visited him. *The council plans to keep its power, and the divine mentor seems to be the mastermind behind it all. With Sinisar as her little minion.*

"Dearest smithing mentor," Lucilia chided. "Fae could never unite when there is such division between male and female. The people's not-so-cherished queen is missing, and have they yet to revolt? It seems our kingdom is primed for change."

A long moment passed before the divine mentor sighed. "I will have you know, our very land is angered by the acts of this male mage. *He* is to blame for recent failures of the kingdom, for fae being led astray. The spirit he embodies has deteriorated our lower sector. And the citizens of Shadow Hills *will* know of this truth, even if they have to see it with their own eyes."

Chortles echoed through the dark tunnel like rattling bones. "And the alchemist? Morian refuses to see the portal's dysfunction."

"In short," she said in her angelic cadence, "our brooding alchemy mentor refuses to change because his tricks work well enough. He reinforces this kingdom's final barrier between the old ways and true divinity."

The squealing brakes ceased. Aramis laid on the rocky floor and closed his eyes. Limbs bunched together as close as they could get to his stomach. He tried his best to breathe with long exhales, pretending to sleep.

"Do you not believe our king was wrong to let the alchemist propose such a lenient punishment?" Sinisar asked. "What if the contestant ends up fixing our compass portal and successfully summoning the Asenath?"

"That will never happen," said the divine voice from the platform outside of the metal bars.

The cell filled with light, pressing onto his closed eyelids.

"Of course not," Sinisar's voice had drastically quieted. "But the council was wrong to vote against me."

"You played your role, Sinisar. Leave the rest to me."

The dry, cold wind inside the mine gave way to unnatural heat; the world a searing red pressure. Aramis wanted to shift and move away, but then he'd be forced to speak with the mentor. Taking a chance, he twisted so his back faced the cell bars. At least he no longer felt the urge to shield his eyes.

"Yes, Lucilia."

"Alert me when you see the others."

Warning bells rang in a quickening staccato pattern, close and loud. The sound pierced his eardrum like a sword. Growing heat burned into his turned back. If he hadn't turned to face the wall, he doubted he would've been able to breathe. A terrible warmth burned its way past his skin, rendering the very muscles in his body hot and tired.

A thick lump stuck in the center of his throat. He couldn't swallow because the light scrutinized every movement. His stomach felt like a bag of hot meat.

Even then, Aramis started to fade away from his body, giving into the bliss of shimmering colors. The red light had turned gold, then white—he couldn't tell whether his eyes were open or closed anymore. It made no difference.

Warm fingers met his back and he jumped, suddenly regaining his sense of where the light ended and his own form began. He scuttled up to the wall.

The light shrank to a floating silhouette in the shape of the divine mentor. Her glow had an innate beauty that tempted him to look into her eyes.

The light unfolded to reveal sights of beautiful waterfalls and naked female fae playing with one another in flowered gardens. The sights changed and morphed the longer he stared. Aramis grew closer to the shapes the more he gazed inside, the deeper he studied. His fear of fixing the compass portal melted away, replaced by a seed of desire—a need to explore the infinite light Lucilia offered. He soon needed nothing more from the outside world, preferring the chasing sense of promise this light provided. Over time, pictures of an alternate future appeared.

He didn't see himself, not exactly. In the vision he was taller, with more well-defined muscles; a worthy competitor in the tournament. A strong fighter, according to the longsword he wielded. Heavy, orcish armor spanned broad shoulders like mountains. It was everything the council wanted him to be. Long dark wings stretched from behind him and without second thought Aramis reached out, though he wasn't sure if he moved his arm at all. He yearned for the image, so eager to leave behind a body ridden with pain and sorrow and inevitable failure.

Green, kind eyes—fuzzy within a blinding glow, ruining his vision —held his attention as they bobbed within tulip fields, up and down, as if pulled along by a wind he couldn't feel. They looked like all-knowing buttons sewn into the fabric of the world just to watch over him for protection.

That sing-song voice returned inside of his head. *All you need is the light...* It said. *What's more important than feeling accepted? Accomplished?*

Those green eyes shined at him, squinting.

I'll tell you anything, the voice said. *Everything you want to know is here, thanks to those who have given themselves to the light before you. Follow their lead.*

Aramis would share everything, as long as this feeling remained.

Sharp, icy pinches burrowed behind his eyes, all the way to the back of his head, but the pain soon disappeared. Aramis couldn't look away from that green gaze as it floated up and down, closer, now in a gleaming sea of nothing but pale yellow.

Closer, he thought. *Please.*

Then darkness consumed everything around those precious green eyes, golden light shrinking down to the outline of Lucilia's usual form. Hopelessness returned inside the dark cell. A terrible sadness fell over him at the prospect of having to save the kingdom, yet being a mean-ingless joke of a mage.

Another part of him thought clearly, growing stronger with every moment he remembered the imp's conversation. He questioned the divine mentor's motives here, how she seemed to prove the imp correct on every level. But it was so difficult to combat the light; as he shifted, he felt his gaze pulled again toward the mentor.

Now Lucilia appeared the same as she had during ceremonies and festivals—an amber-skinned fae with green, shapely features, so perfect she could have been carved from stone. All of her students presented themselves in a similar manner, as if they were tiny twins of her making, all following the way of the light. Aramis had never seen her so close before, and never had he thought a fae so flawless.

No, Aramis thought, pulling his gaze away.

The light still drew closer, pressing in like the midday sun.

She is taking over my mind.

His heart joined the lump in his throat when she knelt to meet the level of his gaze. A rush of creamy vanilla scent fell over him. He sighed, falling into her presence—the close heat. Waving green hair framed her wide and appreciative gaze.

She inched so close they could have kissed. His body felt warm, and a tingling sensation rushed through his legs as his pores opened and he began to sweat.

Lucilia raised a vial within the tiny fraction of space dividing them. Boiling copper liquid stewed inside. "Divine luck," she murmured.

Even if he tried to resist, the female fae caringly whispered, "Go on," which was more than he could possibly ignore. A shaky weakness overcame his limbs. He could hardly grasp the vial.

"For good luck," she said. "And for me?"

"Luck..." The word scraped out against dry lips. He closed his mouth upon realizing it'd been open this whole time.

Luck was always a good thing to jump at, let alone divine luck. He'd be unstoppable with this all-encompassing light on his side.

The liquid in the vial had settled. Steam accumulated in the open space and the cork popped out from sheer pressure, bouncing across damp rock to the other side of the cell. Lucilia's encouraging green eyes never left Aramis, wrinkles piling at the corners.

The need to blink forced Aramis to close his eyes for the slightest moment, wherein he witnessed a shred of darker escape. He managed to tear his gaze away, but the divine fae could not be ignored.

"Drink," she said, her voice like a thousand rays of sunlight working their way to the very core of his soul. The golden glow extended past her fae form once more, brightening to fill the cell. It reeked of burning wood. Wherever he looked, he couldn't escape the divine sight. The light became so hot it turned his breath into a scraping wheeze.

He thought he heard a voice outside telling Lucilia to stop. The light of the room only grew brighter. The heat made him want to tear off his skin.

Nevertheless, his arm began to rise against his will.

The vial tilted back.

He couldn't stop his mouth from opening; his arm shook.

Rusty liquid of a floral scent nearly leaked over the vial onto his lips.

Outside, a voice shouted. "Morian. A pleasure!" The greeting might as well have been a scream.

A torrent of light whirled around Aramis, gathering in fae form near the bars of the cell. Immense pressure subsided from the front of his head and he fell forward, bracing himself against the rocky floor. Somehow, the divine mentor had removed the vial from his hands, though its sticky golden-brown residue remained between his fingers.

When he looked up, Lucilia walked forward, her body split briefly by each one of the cell's bars, amassing once more on the open side and walking out of view. "It is good to see you," she said to the alchemy mentor. "I trust our female contestant has been shipped away?"

Simmia, Aramis thought, his head spinning. He hoped she didn't have to go through whatever just happened to him, losing her self-control entirely and giving herself up to the mentor. Blotchy red spaces took up a good portion of his vision. *What did Lucilia hope to achieve by feeding me that potion?* It couldn't have been his death...

"One might say our kingdom's image is perfectly united," a fourth fae responded. This mentor spoke with a voice so high it reminded him of birdson. *Vis, the elemental mentor*. "I believe no allies will know of this occurrence."

"Possible," Lucilia said. "If we summon this season's Asenath successfully."

A cart door squeaked open. "And the male contestant?" This inquisitive voice certainly belonged to the alchemy mentor.

The only mentor I can trust.

"I've already had the pleasure," Lucilia said, a proud lilt in her voice. "Our gifted mage appears eager to prove his worth."

9

TRANSVERSE PROPERTIES

Aramis received no more than a curt nod from Morian. He emerged from the cell with sore muscles and a sharp pain reaching from the back of his forehead to behind his eyes. Even gazing upon the warm lantern light of the tunnels hurt. He sweat profusely and couldn't seem to get cooler.

Lucilia and Sinisar had insisted Aramis ride in their mine cart on the way to the compass portal, located further beneath the dungeons of the Losamara mines. He'd only ever heard of the compass portal because of its relevance in summoning the future queen, and knew nothing else about the structure.

Cave rock dotted with untapped gems, resources the kingdom of Shadow Hills hadn't yet zoomed by his periphery. Aramis tried tilting his head away from the sight of the divine queen so he wouldn't fall prey to her light once again, though her golden aura seemed to drift and glide with every turn of the cart, like the trails of a torch dragged along at a great speed.

He closed his eyes. *I wonder if Morian knows of the divine queen's attempt to drug me.* It looked like he wouldn't have the chance to ask. Regardless, the alchemist's presence had saved him. Lucilia seemed hesitant to allow her light to shine at the level of brightness it had before, likely because Morian and Vis followed close behind.

Aramis only felt safe when the minecart ground to a stop and he was soon joined by the other two mentors.

A lofty pyramid commanded the open cavern, as tall and wide as the space itself, though it sat in the very back half with a regal, over-looking posture. It didn't seem possible for a piece of fae construction to be so large and intricate this far below ground, and at the same time so old. His eyes trailed down the slick sides, taking in the wide base, melding with the rock floor. The pyramid seemed carved out of the cave itself.

The compass portal?

Despite the foreboding presence, as if something might walk out from the entrance at the very top of the stairs and shoot them down with arrows, the pyramid had to be the most beautiful design the kingdom had ever built. This architecture went beyond basic func-tioning buildings his fellow males aimed to construct. Even the male and female castles, with their tall spires, swirling decorations on the ends, seemed childish and whimsical compared to the solid geomet-rical shape of the compass portal. The pyramid pulsated with a violet glow, imbued with a dark magick Aramis didn't understand.

He couldn't help but feel irresistibly drawn to the structure, but that dark pull also frightened him, signifying the infinite number of realms he could accidentally transport to. The imp's advice to think of a future queen came rushing back, and the prospect of actually summoning someone perfect enough to help restore the kingdom, if he could even conceive of such a being, brought all his excitement to a sudden end. He felt torn between wanting to summon the perfect queen for the kingdom, and the fear of not being capable, given the intricacy of the compass portal. The mentors had set him up to fail, leaving him trapped alone in some desolate realm.

That inviting glow leaked from the stone's cracks and crevices—the same rich violet color Aramis recognized from sconces and the dark mentor.

He also recognized flowers and feathers decorated at the top of waist-high sticks, plotted in front of the pyramid's steps. The layout of the sticks created various paths leading to larger, circular spaces. He smelled a familiar berry scent and craved the Shadow Hills forest, where he felt his most free, and had last seen these flower bulbs while he and they were both considered "wild." Many things lived in that forest, especially under the moonlight, but he'd always thought these bulbs were amongst the most elegant. Here, they'd been plucked from their roots—beheaded—bunched by the hundreds, and skewered on the ends of sticks for the kingdom to use for its advantage. Years of growth thrown away with flair.

I can relate.

The reason for the gathered flora was their shimmering blue light, shining brighter from the help of silver feathers fanned out underneath each bushel. A silvery hue imposed itself upon every nook of the wide cavern. Aramis searched for a sign of Erlick, but the winged, furry little imp was nowhere in sight.

A center path formed by the bulbed flowers led straight toward the pyramid's steps. The monumental stone stairs leading up the pyramid's front entrance might as well have been worshipped in their own right. To climb up one of the tall steps, Aramis would need the jumping skills of Inebrius the Agile, or the stride of a giant.

Sinisar and Lucilia strode down paths separated by the different clusters of the glowing pathway, taking up positions at two of the four clearings inside the cave. Mentors began carefully inspecting large totems inside their respective clearings.

Morian, along with the sterilizing scent of alchemy, appeared like a ghost at Aramis's side. His eyes studied the winding path on their left, leading to a clearing filled with hundreds of miniature alchemical tables like the ones they'd used in class. He rested a heavy hand on Aramis's shoulder.

"Can you fix this portal and summon the queen?" The mentor's expressionless mood sucked the remaining hope from Aramis and replaced it with a harsh embrace of reality.

I must take this opportunity to try to summon the Asenath, Aramis thought. *The only other option is to cower, admit defeat, and remain in this underground mine forever.*

I have to try, despite what might happen.

"Fae are arrogant," Morian the alchemist said. "I think you stand a chance. No matter what the others say."

Morian's warning sounded familiar. Was it Erlick who had last warned him of the fatal flaw of pride? Aramis struggled to remember. The lingering pain in his head from Lucilia's divine light made following any line of thought as difficult as conjuring from other realms. If any shred of focus remained in his exhausted state, he wanted to save it for summoning the Asenath.

"Walk to the steps," Morian said in a quick whisper. "No further." He strode down the leftmost pathway.

Aramis walked the remaining path to the pyramid steps. He did his best to avoid staring into the violet glow, wary of whatever might tempt him since the divine mentor's light. From a position in front of the first step, which was taller than he stood, Aramis turned to see the mentors in their respective clearings marked by the glowing stick. Sinisar stood amidst a hundred anvils no larger than what would be used to craft a king's goblet. They looked like black dwarven coffins.

A natural—albeit miniature—forest surrounded the elemental mentor in the fourth clearing. Green shrubbery clawed at her ankles as she wandered, circling her totem pole.

Morian appeared comfortable in his element. It was likely he'd be able to conduct satisfactory alchemical work with an audience if it weren't for the shrunken size of the tables around him; not to mention waist-high shelves that stored miniature ingredients Aramis recognized as cuts of witheroot and its spindly leaves and the rare, flesh-eating heads of *Comisarius Potheitus*.

Rare, why? Because it came from another realm. He'd studied up on the plant in the little free time he'd had with magickal texts, fearing that time may not be enough. Imagine if he ended up in a world full of flesh-eating bulbous plants, capable of using their roots to slither along the ground, climb and reach, wrapping him in thorned vines and drinking his blood like water.

Aramis wished to rid himself of this vague state between wanting to prove himself and the fear of other realms, feeling as if his stomach might leap out of his throat. But all he could do was push on and ignore those thoughts telling him he wasn't enough. He may be set up for failure, according to the mentors and his fellow contestants, but it was better to try to prove them wrong than spend the short remainder of his life wallowing the mines—or worse, escaping from vines.

Lucilia strode happily atop a pile of white sand. The occasional wave of pebbles stirred with the cave's stale wind. Three light beams stood from ceiling to sand as thin, mostly imperceptible towers of golden light. Aramis glanced all of this before forcing himself to divert his gaze from Lucilia's piercing eyes, the most mesmerizing force in the room. He wouldn't be strong enough to defend himself if he fell under her spell once again.

He followed Morian's advice to stay off the pyramid's first step while repeating the advice Erlick told him about dark magick to help summon the queen.

Think about the natural qualities of a queen. Qualities only I can imagine.

But these thoughts quickly gave way to nervous glances and the realization that the mentors, who would also be hosting the tournament games, had split into four separate spaces of the cavern, occupying vague circles filled with miniature items that resembled the four male skills.

There are four games in every tournament, he reminded himself. *A clearing and a game for every mentor?* He even had pre-tournament jitters, unable to stand remotely still. Say he did successfully summon the Asenath and was able to compete in the tournament, knowing the games meant he'd be able to plan accordingly, and improve his chances of winning.

"My dear armory mentor..." Lucilia lowered her glow to a radiating light that hardly shone past her skin. "Perhaps you'd like to begin? After all, we are here on account of your castle's inadequacies."

"Delighted." Sinisar's demeanor remained stiff and calculated. He shuffled amongst the tiny anvils, muttering to himself.

He meandered back to a particular anvil he had inspected for some time.

The mentor removed a curved sword from a sheath hanging at his waist. The sound of sharpened steel rang throughout the cave. The blade's incarnadine aura emanated from a pattern of runes carved into the metal, visible only after filling with light.

The imp said Aramis would never have a chance at winning the traditional tournament—a point he couldn't agree with more, unless he studied up now. The art of smithing had felt clunky to him since the first time he struck his finger with a hammer. Just seeing the equipment in use made him uncomfortable, but if smithing meant being able to change the kingdom's beliefs for good, then he would pick up a hammer.

Sinisar sat atop a barrel next to the anvil he selected. From a set of nearby smithing equipment, he chose a tiny smithing hammer. The mentor looked odd wielding the toy-like weapon given the gaudy design of his cloak and decorated armor, adorned with precious metals symbolizing awards he himself had created. It seemed as if he'd attempted to garner respect throughout his entire life. His mannerisms were so easy to mock, and maybe that wasn't his fault, but a result of caring too much.

When he rested the blade on the anvil, shoulders back, he confidently lifted the tiny hammer. He struck the blade once with the nonchalance of a launderer hanging clothes. Years of study seemed behind the single stroke.

A ringing note pierced through the air, triggering a much lower hum coming from behind Aramis—inside the pyramid. The honeyed tone of a struck gong that wouldn't end. A dull baritone, magnifying the pyramid's violet aura.

Aramis shuffled on the platform before the pyramid steps. The surrounding area developed a vibration that numbed his feet.

Meanwhile, his chest felt hollow. This tournament was so much bigger than him. His hands tightened at the thought of what this might have meant for Morian, who went against the council's initial verdict and defended Aramis whenever possible. If he failed, he'd be letting down the alchemy mentor, along with everyone else forced to serve because they didn't fit the mold of a traditional craft.

Bitter hatred replaced all else when Sinisar waved his red blade in the air with intricate, warrior-proving movements.

Lucilia rolled her eyes and the elemental mentor giggled.

Sinisar knelt in front of the wooden carved totem, its dessicated bark resembling the reddest of pine trees. The armory mentor held his sword at the mid-torso, check position. A thin whipping slice through the air, and he struck a gash across the statue's beautiful carvings.

Profanity, Aramis thought. The slightest damage to any sacred structure in Shadow Hills called for three public lashings, at minimum. He searched around, ready for a mentor to shout at the debasing of this magickal structure, it appeared that everyone watched on, transfixed as the totem developed a violet hue deeper than the pyramid's, rising steadily up the totem with the billowing consistency of a distant cloud.

So that is the first game? It seems we only have to craft a sword, and then use it...

Sinisar twisted on his heels, spinning his sword deftly before tucking it back into his curved leather sheath. "Lucilia?" he said, sarcasm ridden throughout his tone. "I trust you have confidence that the great pyramid will accept each one of your castle's conceited games. Let us see you demonstrate the next one."

Aramis found it necessary to risk eye contact so he could study the divine mentor's process of lighting her totem.

The divine mentor moved with a calm confident precision. Unlike the brisk walk of Morian, her movements had a certain cadence and dance in her step, soon fluttering with golden wings through the air to gracefully touch all three beams of light within her clearing. Gently and easily, the towers faded away, and when her hand touched the final band, a glowing stag appeared. The stag, made of nothing other than white ether, pranced over the mounds of sand.

The mentor made a swift movement, throwing an object out from her hip—a translucent dagger spun through the air and thudded into the deer's vital organs. A perfect hit, stealthy and impossible to counter. The stag squealed its way into death as if it weren't made of her divine light.

Aramis could relate to the animal's agonizing scream, the pressure the beast must have felt as Lucilia stood overhead, ending its misery.

The divine mentor emerged from her crouch holding its long head by the antlers. The animal's tongue stuck out with a bright clear liquid dripping from the flat end. The same unemotional look on the stag also occupied her face.

Aramis swallowed a lump in his throat. *Is this what awaits me if I go against the rest of the council?* It wasn't impossible to determine what this game tested for, however. The male skill of hunting was clearly present, but it wasn't clear why Lucilia would include totems of light unless she meant to distract contestants.

The divine mentor dropped the stag's head at the far end of her designated clearing, near the totem. She dipped her finger into glowing white blood, dripping onto the cave floor as she painted over the painted totem. In moments, she stepped back to admire what looked like a ten-year-old's drawing of a stag.

Yet, the violet hue soared to illuminate the wooden sculpture, and the hum of the pyramid brightened to a chorus of two notes—a second high-pitch tone to join the first that remained low.

A painting of a stag? Once again, Aramis doubted whether these rituals had anything to do with the tournament at all.

Her back turned, Lucilia said, "Morian... The fabled prince of alchemical crafts. Care to show us your tournament game? It is a shame our dark mentor is not here to make the presentation herself."

"I trust in Celeste." Morian searched carefully amidst shelves filled with bristly leaves, vials not quite unlike what Lucilia held in the dungeon, hard to identify cuts of meat, and bowls of powder in nearly every color except for the one he appeared to need. Aramis knew of many possible combinations using these ingredients, but what would a tournament game require contestants to create? A potent love potion? A cure for a contracted illness? Or would they be tasked to play with the transmutation of living organisms?

Arms brimming with vials, Morian made his way to a collection of two small tables. He lowered ingredients into the cauldron with careful consideration. Reactions took place inside of the pot, but the mentor seemed displeased.

Unfamiliar, twisting forms that emerged from the cauldron's reactions, evaporating as they stretched into the world of the living.

The alchemy mentor backed away, tossing flecks of red powder into the pot from a distance. Clouds of smoke leapt into the air, dousing shelves and the unused cauldrons in a thick plume as it settled.

Morian limped out of the fog. Odd squeals arose behind him.

Disturbed, animalistic shouts ricocheted off the cave walls. A third vibration oscillated between the two hums of the pyramid.

Even Lucilia, the divine mentor, looked around as if trying to make sense of Morian's act. She spoke through her teeth. "Quite the show you've displayed."

Morain gaze a wheezing cough. "You've seen nothing."

A white crow no bigger than a rat sat perched upon the cauldron's edge, tilting its head to peer through glowing sticks, shaking and stretching its wings.

Morian whispered to the animal, too soft for Aramis to understand, though the syllables echoed throughout the cave.

The crow tilted its head as it understood and flew to the very top of the totem pole. A cloud of purple essence trailed behind, illuminating the third totem of the cavern. Then the albino crow spiraled from the ceiling's stalagmites down into the totem to disappear.

Aramis lowered his head and searched his memory for any alchemical test that included white crows. He could find none, at a loss when it came to finding the meaning of this third game.

Lucilia quickly spoke over the spectacle. "Decent alignment with our intentions."

Sinisar let out a pitiful laugh. After glancing at Aramis, the mentor stood straighter. "I'd prefer if we jump upon this opportunity our gracious realm has offered. Vis, have you prepared?"

Near the last, unlit totem, the elemental mentor spoke in a high-pitched voice filled with wonder. "I believe so."

Vis's manner had a laziness that lacked any real composure or sign of intention. Surrounded by trees, it wasn't entirely clear what the elemental mentor had planned for her tournament game. Vis used her thin green wings to flutter through the dense forest in her area. It seemed as if she were only brushing the trees with her fingers until they began to grow rapidly behind her. Branches reached up to the mentor like praising hands in a rush to touch her floating feet.

Aramis wondered what the male role could possibly be in a game that manipulated trees—a skill belonging to elemental, female magick. Other tasks from the mentor's games—make the best weapon, hunt the stag, create *something* using alchemical ingredients—all made sense, but what could a male do in a forest of trees?

Build, perhaps?

Vis reached down and plucked a leaf from one of the trees she stood upon, placing it carefully on top of the totem to douse the tower in a purple aura.

A deep groan came from the pyramid. After a short silence, the hums returned louder than ever, a chorus of droning, buzzing tones that vibrated in Aramis's chest. At the top of the steps, a pillar of stone slid aside to reveal a dark passageway—the grinding of rock terribly slow.

A golden ray appeared, shining past Aramis, over his left shoulder. The divine mentor's wind-chime voice sang into his ear. "Sinisar?"

"Right away."

The young fae shuddered when Sinisar pulled himself onto the first step of the pyramid, climbing all the way to the fourth. He waited for something to happen to the mentor, for some bomb that Morian planted to explode, but nothing.

Sinisar left a tiny red sphere on the edge of the fourth step. The red in the sphere's center soon grew darker and more full. Aramis spotted a form inside. It looked like some sort of fetus growing inside of a transparent egg. He soon recognized the face as impish—a gross, demonic thing with horns and a maniacal smile stretching all the way to its ears.

The sphere cracked along its side. The red form trapped in a slimy bubble emerged from its shell, sliding down the few steps in a secondary, thin casing.

It seemed as if the creature tried to speak or groan, but the remaining coat of residue covering the imp made a respectable barrier. The creature tore at the shell with a pointed fingernail and broke free.

Tiny red wings wiggled and twitched on its back as the imp struggled to prop one leg up and come to its wobbly feet. "Damn summoning process... A ride through the flaming realms is what it is."

Aramis was thinking the same thing. Would traveling to the Asenath's realm be this shameful? He didn't want to make his first impression to the future queen to be him emerging from some interrealm womb.

"Welcome to the fae realm of Shadow Hills." Lucilia separated herself from the other mentors by taking a brisk step. "May I have your name?"

"*Mmm.*" The imp finally managed to stand straight, rubbing its head and rotating its arms. Little red hairs laid slick over his gut. "Thank you for asking. Erlick, it is." As the imp scanned everyone in the room, he took no additional notice of Aramis. "It is a pleasure that you call on Imp Services. Pardon my asking, but word from my realm is that fae aren't having a tournament this season. So, to avoid beating around your realm's metaphorical bush, what is the need for me exactly?" This polite version of Erlick made Aramis even more doubtful. This same pressing imp that visited his cell and told him of the mentor's schemes.

"Strange rumors," Morian said. "May I ask where an imp heard such words?"

"Mentor," Lucilia turned quickly with a beat of her wings. "Is it not normal for rumors to arise when our queen is missing?"

"Are you referring to our current queen?" Morian asked. "Or the queen we have yet to summon for this season? *Ah*, never mind... I'm not certain it matters."

"The grandest delicacy in all of the realms." Erlick tapped his six fingers against one another. "A fae disagreement. Do you know what that means? Conflict, lies, broken hearts... reunion, strife, and the tiniest bit of positive outcome."

Even Aramis knew it wasn't wise to make fun of the council's ways —an unspoken law of the kingdom.

"Apologies if I offended, but imps love seeing the ways of all of the realms. It's part of why we tolerate... I mean, appreciate, you fae. You are so unique."

"No such thing as a broken heart would ever exist in this kingdom. And this is not a disagreement." The divine queen seemed to pronounce every word carefully.

The imp raised his hands in the air as if not guilty.

"We are in a state of change," she continued. "Love is in the air, yet our compass cannot sense it. That is why we need you."

The imp turned and began to take stock of Aramis. It felt like being judged for a role in the local troupe. In a way, Aramis felt he was acting, playing the role of a capable mage until the time came to prove himself. "Who is this one? He is scared."

"This is the fae you will accompany if the portal is functional. You two will venture into the realm of the Asenath and bring her to us."

"*Greeat.*" The imp rolled his eyes. "Another traveling gig. I imagine there will be no per diem, either?"

"I'm sorry," Vis said with the nimblest voice to ever pass through the air. "Can we summon a different imp?"

"You couldn't find a more reliable imp if you tried," Erlick said. "I understand. You can't find the Asenath for this precious season, and this random contestant is your last hope. This stuff happens. If he *actually* manages to find your queen, which you don't seem too sure about, you'll need me, the real guns, to bring the two of them back. Can't count on an idiot hundred-something to convince the most beautiful female in all the realms, can we?"

"Y-yes," said the divine queen. "I mean, no."

"On with it." Morian gestured to the stairs. "The portal needs direction."

The imp jumped, clapping thrice. Its wings fluttered rapidly as it lowered to the ground. "How great. An actual task to complete."

A weak red hand gripped Aramis on the arm. As the imp's skin touched his, the world swirled into a vortex and the scene changed, his footing shifting to the left. A force gently pulled at his right arm, nudging him to proper balance within a dark room that had the powdery stench of accumulated dust.

But the world wouldn't stop spinning in his head, and Aramis dropped to his knees to avoid being sick. "What was that?"

"*What was that?*" The imp repeated in a timid voice. "Stand up if you want to do anything for your kingdom. We're at the top of the pyramid. Here, come this way. I think the portal is on our left."

🦋 10 🦋

MENTAL MIRROR

J agged stone walls echoed every gruff syllable Aramis heard from the imp. Sconces along the ceiling emitted a radiant shimmer upward, their height and glow giving an otherworldly feel to the pyramid's inner room. The walls and very floor itself appeared upside down and out of place.

Three arched openings stretched from the floor to the ceiling—one in front of Aramis, one on his left, and one on his right. Behind each opening was a large stone wall, so he'd have to walk into the archways and around the walls to discover what lay deeper inside the pyramid. Perhaps a fae trained in dark magick could understand the symbols carved in the rock above each passageway, but Aramis only knew the most basic of spells. Even when he did get his hands on an advanced magical text, the looping sentences and references nested in past lessons meant little to him.

The leftmost carving contained an innate glow. It was the shape of two straight lines, like pillars within an oval. A violet hue shone out of that carving, so much like the light from the totems that the two somehow had to be connected. He noticed how concentrated the music sounded near the left archway.

"I can't believe this is the portal," Erlick said.

The statement drew Aramis out of the trance cast upon him.

"My brother Clarick would give his right wing to see this—an actual human. You're in for a lot. A whole lot of despair within love, that is." The imp let out a bellyful of chuckles. "I never would have thought a human would be this year's Asenath, given the state of Earthrealm."

"The Asenath is not from a good land? Surely it can't be worse than our kingdom?" Perhaps there had been a fatal flaw in the summoning process already. What help would the Asenath be if she came from a corrupted realm? The kingdom needed someone with solutions, who knew how a working kingdom thrived and could re-create that in a realm of magick, bringing the entire kingdom with them.

"Why else would I say you're in for a lot? Cheer up. It's not all bad. Many things that plague humans can be found in your very kingdom. You may relate on more levels than one, and I trust in the wisdom of the compass portal."

"Then I don't see how she can help us. A corrupt Asenath would only feed the kingdom more lies."

"Oh no. Don't think they're anywhere near as corrupt as the fae. We imps benefit from your society because fae are too busy squabbling with each other to manage their menial tasks. We use magick to handle them for you, and kindly take your payments. Humans thought it better to eliminate us. No hard feelings, of course. We always knew the rejection of magick would come back to bite them. That wasn't the first time they cast away their magickal nature, and it won't be the last."

As a male fae taught nothing but the craft of smithing, ideas of history—especially that of other realms—wasn't a part of what Aramis studied while prepping for the tournament games. History was yet another craft deemed unverifiable, and therefore secondary. He remembered humanity's stories being told around the fire at night, no more than silly fables holding a kernel of truth. Cautionary tales. Never in his life did he consider meeting a human, let alone electing one as his queen. The way the imp spoke of them didn't make him wildly enthusiastic, either. "Are they... dumb?"

"Not dumb, per se. Magickally disinclined? Spiritually inept? Ignorant and skeptical? Most definitely."

Aramis considered the possibility of meeting a new creature so hopelessly unfamiliar with magick. Summoning such a queen didn't make sense; he'd dedicated his life to the four female crafts. His mate should've been another mage, more skilled than himself. It would only make sense to have someone who understood his passions. "How does the portal know I would fare best with a human? I haven't even begun thinking about her qualities yet. I've been waiting for the portal, like you told me. Why would I want such a creature if they're so ungrounded?"

"You'll see," Erlick said, which made Aramis feel worse. How was he supposed to summon a human to rebuild the realm when all he knew of the species was their flaws?

"Humans are naturally beautiful," said the imp, holding a finger in the air as he made his point. "You know, they have a sense of community that's unique to their realm, so genuine, so intertwined, that if you look into their eyes, you see the souls of their ancestors... Or so they say. I've never met one."

"Yeah." Aramis nodded, familiar with the myth. Seeing the past lives of fae just by looking into their eyes sounded distracting. Besides, humans weren't supposed to be much different than the fae. "Legend also says they live short lives. How should I account for this? The future queen would hardly live the length of her ruling season. She is but an inexperienced being. From where do we expect her to draw her wisdom? Her ancestors? And never mind her getting along with the fae council..."

Aramis couldn't help but chuckle at the poor likelihood of him ever loving a magickless human. The poor likelihood of that this summoning would succeed.

"If the compass portal chose Earthrealm, so be it," Erlick said. "Sometimes two opposites make a whole, some people say. Point is, this is not the first time a human has been chosen. If I'm not mistaken, I believe the Asenath of the twenty-seventh season was one of those creatures lacking magick."

Aramis reached into the furthest depths of his memories, surprised by what he grasped. Perhaps he learned a little history from those campfire stories after all. "Patra, the Queen of Roses? She was a human?"

"That's her. See? You should be excited to meet one of her kind."

Aramis struggled to find such a positive feeling as he followed the imp. Why even try his luck with the portal when he'd summon an incapable queen? He didn't believe in the portal's abilities no matter what the imp or some dark textbook claimed.

Erlick pattered around the corner of the left arch on feet much too large for his stature. "You two will be more than fine. Both of you have a will to do whatever you want. Do you remember how the twenty-seventh Asenath earned her name, the Queen of Roses?"

"She could summon roses from any realm." Patra was credited with saving an orc village beyond the forest from their aggressive neighbors by planting orange roses in the wildlands. The roses had scents akin to freshly seasoned meat, with petals so voluminous they could turn the mind of any head-splitting veteran into that of a pacifist priest. No alchemist or magickal practitioner had been able to recreate or locate such roses ever since. The slogan of her reign came to Aramis's mind.

"A rose is never just a rose," he uttered.

As he rounded the corner with shaking legs, the sheer violet light of the compass portal— undoubtedly the object before him—reached out and wrapped him in an embrace of ever-loving, cool air, brushing over his skin like the fresh ocean breeze.

He'd never seen light move as slowly as the light coming out of the portal. Every strand wriggled through the air, seeking him. It was as if the purple hue from the totems accumulated in this back room of the pyramid, clumping together to form a physical mass out of nothing but the mix of foggy violet light—a bubbling love potion or haunted lake in the night, standing vertically. Aramis gazed into the ebb and flow of the portal's light, the dense center.

An image of Simmia came to mind.

His skin tingled at the memory of her eager embrace.

Satin sheets.

A dark room with heavy breathing.

He let a free hand take in every inch of her curving body, so soft.

The arch of her back gave into him.

He was on top of her with nothing to cover.

Her dress came off slowly, a sight that he savored, and when their bare skin touched, an electric spell filled him with all the energy of the realm.

He tamed the rising flame within him with gentle kisses on her velvet skin, between her thighs, where she was sweet. He licked ever-so-softly and she trembled, clutching him beneath the arms and pulling him up—gripping the length of him with one hand.

He hadn't noticed how hard he'd been for her.

She rubbed the tip of him against her wetness and he thrust forward with a deep grunt, to which she moaned, and her lower back arched once more while she twisted and pulled at the sheets around her, exposing the skin of her neck for Aramis to bite.

Her eyes rolled back beneath fluttering lids, mouth opening in a wordless gasp as he throbbed—

"Focus," Erlick said, his voice distant and complaining. "If you're teleported to some random realm because you can't keep focused, I'm *not* coming after you."

"I..." Aramis shook his head—shocked out of passionate reverie, a daydream that felt much too real. He stared at the portal's swirling light from a few steps away.

The resonant hum warbled through him. Sonic pulses struck as low vibrations in his chest. It felt as if the pyramid deliberately played with his sensations.

If anything, the portal seemed to know more about what he wanted than he did. The most soothing instrument in all the realms played the tune of a perfect memory from his own heart.

"Didn't you say you were coming with me?" he asked the imp with a shaky voice he couldn't hide. Aramis swallowed, mouth having gone terribly dry. He hadn't taken his gaze away from the shifting lights.

"I said that we must fix the portal, and I warned you about the dangers of dark magick. What else? Do you want me to know the exact logistics of how every portal in every realm works? I'm an imp, not some codex of universal information. I told you everything you need to do, all I know, and now the rest is up to you."

All Aramis wanted was to live a good life with his future mate. To love and be loved for the mage he was. Must he risk his life to do so? Not to mention his existence in a sane fae realm, the presence of his wings, and a chance to compete in the tournament.

If he didn't try this, he'd be giving everything up to the mentors and Lucilia. The one who drugged him, and according to the imp, planned some big conspiracy to stay in power. Whatever the case, this was Aramis's lot, and if he didn't move forward, he felt the entire realm would never progress.

Taking a deep breath, Aramis tried to ready himself for the imagery and seduction the compass portal would evoke. Rather than focus on the past and everything he could lose, the incompatibility of the human being, he needed to remember his concept of the perfect future queen.

The portal's rays changed pattern, circling toward the dense center in a hypnotic swirl.

Familiar warmth returned to his chest, the sensation from when he first discovered his love for the craft of magick. His appreciation never arose from a specific intention to be a mage, or because he wanted to be the greatest mage in the world, but out of love for the craft itself. He focused on these feelings.

Walking home from a late sparring occasion.

It was windy, which bothered him because it was also frigid and that combination always seemed to make it difficult to breathe. The wind forced him to walk sideways to catch his breath. That put him in a bad mood and from a lack of concentration, he'd slipped on a sword in training that day.

What would it be like if the sword punctured right through him?

What would he have seen?

In the distance, a creature wearing an all-black robe.

Walk forth, *it whispered, curling a boney finger.*

The hum of the portal turned high and sweet, as if whistled by the lips of the Queen of Roses herself.

Never had a painting or seeing orb captured how Aramis felt with such exactitude as the compass portal did then. This was the true power of dark magick, and it seemed strange that everyone in the kingdom wasn't practicing a craft capable of reliving memories. The portal's daydreams had been intense, but Aramis wanted to see more.

He wanted to see what the intention of seeing the perfect future queen might yield.

What if he could discover how to deliver this magick to the rest of the kingdom? Five minutes in front of this portal, where a fae's true thoughts and feelings would reflect like a mental mirror, and the council would reach conclusions that might have taken ages to debate.

That's all I want, Aramis thought. *To understand...*

Testing day for male and female castles.

Standing before council members with no particular gift, Aramis's entire worth was to be judged this very moment. If he failed, the opportunities his parents had sacrificed for him to come to Shadow Hills would be for nothing.

Disappointed expressions from council members, mocking faces from class-mates, and a win through a loophole in the qualifying system. His sneaky magick saved him in the form of a dark magick spell, one which he couldn't conjure today, despite the many times he'd tried.

That night, someone had gathered a thousand little auseq caterpillars and thrown them into his bed chambers as revenge. Their terrible white bites itched for days, puss leaking as they healed. He wondered if he'd made the right decision by trying to compete in the tournament, or if he should have gone back home—

"Woah, woah, woah," a voice said. Small hands tugged at his leg. The portal's hum came back to him as Aramis pulled his gaze away, eyes burning with dry heat. He blinked and wiped his tears. It took a moment to remember he was in this dark pyramid.

"See? Do you see what I mean? You *have* to be careful, lest you end up somewhere dark and depressing. Didn't I tell you to be careful? But here you go, losing yourself in the first thing you see. Who cares if you're a natural mage, curious about the world. Do you know how many lives unchecked curiosity has claimed? I'm sure this portal itself has known a few. And I guarantee the compass will *never* point toward the Asenath if you don't at least try to think about her qualities. All I see in your face is shameful fae regret."

Aramis rubbed his throbbing temples. "I know," he managed to mumble, lips fat and heavy. "It was my fault. But there's no way... No way for me to fight the portal calls. I can't do this."

THE BORDER BETWEEN
REALMS

"Do you not remember what I told you to think about?" Erlick's ruby eyes narrowed on Aramis.

Aramis steadied his breath in front of the shimmering portal. "You told me to imagine what I desire in a future queen. To think of unique qualities only fae of my time could imagine." The sheer effort of avoiding the colorful depths of the compass portal required every sliver of focus. He swallowed a lump in his throat, shaking.

How could he consider what the realm needed in a future Asenath in this state? Every thought seemed vital and full of awe, worthy of contemplation. How would he resist exploring his most precious memories when they arose again, tempting him with the intimate embrace of nostalgia?

All he knew was that if he could focus and summon the Asenath, he would avoid losing his soul in a distant realm. He must return to Shadow Hills with the future queen and keep hold of his chance at becoming king and changing the ways of the kingdom for good, however small that chance became.

I have to do my part.

He found a sense of freedom in the narrowed purpose and nurtured the feeling as he approached the compass portal once more. Rather than being caught inside a ray of light and yet another memory, he stared intently into the portal's dense center, where light accumulated into a shining white orb.

Somewhere far away, Erlick advised caution... But Aramis narrowed his eyes in focus.

A new queen needs to change the very beliefs of the kingdom.

She must be capable of withstanding the harshest criticism while maintaining a clear mind. A leader who puts the needs of the fae before her own. The needs of the kingdom before her own. If the human truly is incapable of magick, she must be willing to admit her flaws, as I will mine, and learn those crafts she does not favor.

In his heart, Aramis knew he wanted more. He feared selfishness, but the imp's words

And she must be beautiful. More beautiful than the mentors in both her looks and actions. Above all, she must have a capacity for magick... If humans are unfamiliar, then she must be able to learn.

The irony of desiring the Asenath to learn magick wasn't missed as Aramis contemplated his lack of smithing skills, and how such inadequacies led him here in the first place. Perhaps he shouldn't have judged the future queen so harshly. He peered deeper into the light, stepped closer, and focused on the ambitious hope in his chest that told him maybe, just maybe, a future Asenath such as he imagined existed.

Surrounding violet rays fell away from the center, guiding his gaze back to the orb's edge. He found himself drifting into a memory of the past, practicing basic magick in the forest near moonlit trees.

Focus.

The portal hummed. Aramis heard shifting syllables in the tone, speaking words of an ancient language he couldn't discern. He brought his focus again to the qualities of his Asenath.

She must also be strong enough to walk a lonely path and kind enough to practice empathy.

The highest note within the portal chimed repetitively. A drumming instrument so naturally gracious and welcoming played a steadier beat of lower tones around him. The deep resonance fed violet, beige, and golden-orange colors into the center orb.

Then the orb split into two spheres connected only at their top, darkening in color and lengthening into twists like spindles or braids, still gaining depth. Surrounded by swirling colors of all kinds, the orb —no longer a portal before him, but a painting for Aramis to walk into —took the shape of a head.

Aramis knew it to be his queen.

The shadow elongated, showing the curved body of a wingless being so like the fae, her hands behind her back, chin tilted upward as if studying him. The silhouette had an attractive pull that mimicked the portal's light. Or perhaps, the light mimicked the being. Both seemed to consist of the other.

The portal suggested the form without wholly presenting the Asenath to him. A vague figure drifted back as Aramis stepped further inside. He reached out and clenched thin air, trying to understand this outlined beauty and why he knew her to be his queen.

There is no way to be sure...

Even if she is, a queen so perfect would never return my love.

I'll inevitably lose the tournament.

I lack the necessary skills.

The portal's various lights encapsulated him and the world had no direction. High and low notes continued to ring, adopting no real rhythm until the swirling lights finally settled into recognizable shapes and colors.

All at once, the chimes and hums of the pyramid became the chirps of afternoon birds and a distant mechanical buzz. White from inside the orb took a wavy gray form on the ground—old snow. A fiberglass screen enclosed the space around him, pretending to separate him from the outside world and its frigid breeze. This was where the rest of the portal's color settled, forming what he found to be the most ridiculous excuse for a wall. Aramis shivered, pulling up the hood of his cloak.

A comically small wicker table stood directly in front of his legs, accompanied by chairs with red cushions that hardly reached his waist.

There was no cookware on the undecorated stone floor, and the only place for storage seemed to be a little black box in the far corner.

She can't be here... Not my queen.

He couldn't even have traveled to the realm of humans. Humans didn't have any female crafts, so they would need to be skilled in the male craft of architecture to survive. This home showed nothing of the sort.

He looked in every direction twice. No human was near. Even more sobering was the fact that Erlick had yet to speak his mind unnecessarily, which meant he probably traveled to some desolate realm, where he would never be saved.

Within moments, his overwhelming excitement turned into a crippling feeling of loneliness. *I failed. I entered some random realm and failed my kingdom.*

There was no telling what Lucilia would accomplish by remaining in the queen's place or what the kingdom would be like in the coming years. He resisted looking around to see what awaited him, but curiosity and a desire to get somewhere warmer, inside actual walls, eventually won over.

The home seemed well-off for a peasant or even someone from the lower district, but no future queen would live in such cramped quarters. The residence couldn't have been more than a few bounds wide, attached to another space, visible through a pane of glass.

Aramis and his subpar skills teleported him to some subpar realm. He thought he had a chance at changing Shadow Hills for the better, but the mentors knew he lacked the necessary skills to summon the future queen. That was why they let him use the portal in the first place, predicting him to fail and never be seen again. The imp simply put too much faith in him.

Maybe I thought too much of Simmia.

A half-empty garnet drink sat atop the wicker table, its clear glass shaking from the wind. The air was cold and dirty in his lungs despite being crisper than the mine. This was polluted air. He sniffed toward the attached segment behind him and experienced the one pleasant sensation of the realm thus far—a faint whiff of white vanilla...

He wanted to chase the scent, but halted at the sight of the imp, its wings fluttering in a red blur overhead.

Erlick rubbed his chin while inspecting the poorer home with studious intent. "So..." He ran a finger along the glass window's edge, crumpling the accumulated dust into a ball, then flicking it. "This is it, huh?"

"There is no Asenath here."

"You can't be sure..."

"How can I not? Look around you." Aramis was tired of the imp's optimism.

"I mean, this *is* Earthrealm."

"It is?"

"Undoubtedly. I can smell a lingering human scent. It's..." His nose twitched, sniffing three distinct spots in the air. He shivered. "Like onion. But I don't see any humans around. Guess we'll have to wait."

"Wait..." The word slipped from Aramis's mouth with the weight of lost hope. Desperate, he peered again through the glass window, where a kitchen table stood restlessly in the corner living space, capable of feeding no more than a few mouths. "If this is Earthrealm, then we have not found the queen. The owner of this residence is of no nobility."

"Trust me," Erlick said. "We are looking for a queen in our realm, not theirs. The humans rarely see their own beauty, let alone that of their neighbor. The portal is supposed to drop us in the *exact* location of the future queen. We're a little early, is all."

"What do you mean early?" Aramis asked. "We were supposed to retrieve the Asenath and leave. It was supposed to be a quick operation. Here and back."

"And you may have, as the humans say, 'jumped the gun,'" Erlick said. "You got the space right, but not the time. *My rocks.* So pushy. You're gonna need quite the help impressing this human, I can tell. The realms don't magically bend according to fae whim, you know. If anyone knows, it should be you... prisoner." The imp crossed his arms and fluttered onto a nearby wicker seat, facing away from the glass window.

Aramis sat on the opposite chair. "How long do we wait?"

"Has anyone ever told you that you're an impatient fool?"

Aramis grunted.

"Just sit here and look for me when she arrives. I'll tell you what to say. All you gotta do is follow my lead. Your naivete to this whole enterprise will still be slightly apparent, and we would like to hide those core fae flaws when persuading the future Asenath. I can see your pride better than you."

"My flaws are merely—"

"Yea, yea, yea—your flaws are your strengths." The imp moved one of his bulbed fingers in a circle as if he'd heard this all before. "Save it for the queen."

The creaking of a door stopped the coming argument. Then the hard slam as it shut on the other side of the glass. Shouts came from the left of the kitchen.

Aramis prepared for confrontation. *I needn't kill anything unless it attacks me.* Another yip, and this time he could hear an animal's pure excitement.

A furry white creature ran along the wood floor, four legs frantically slipping in an effort to teleport to the door. Crazed intent raged through the creature's wide eyes. The pudgy frame suggested it ate well with minimal need for strenuous hunting.

It plans to alert the owner of our presence.

Aramis's breaths turned short and any confidence he may have had vanished. It suddenly didn't seem so ridiculous that he'd soon meet his queen and have to convince her to leave the only realm she had ever known, falling in love with an odd creature she'd never seen.

How did the mentors do it before him?

They never considered the will of the Asenath. They simply swapped her old fate for a new, and demanded acceptance.

He'd be asking her to believe in creatures her kind cast aside long ago. Even Erlick said the humans despised magick.

❧ 12 ❧

ILLUSIONS

"As an active member of the teacher's union…" The words caught in her throat. Her voice quivered. Years of frustration neared the verge of eruption. Add in the wine from last night and nothing but a Dunkin' Donuts coffee for breakfast, and she found it impossible to hold back her anger any longer. "I couldn't disagree with you more."

Her words hovered amidst the silence like an old party balloon. Gasps arose around her from fellow teachers who realized she was finally done with the shit.

She couldn't take it anymore.

She never would've said anything, preferring *not* to look like a bitch who lost her mind, but the president of the Dakoma County's school board stopped his oh-so-eloquent speech with the claim that Rhea looked as if she "had something to say," pointing her out in the front row.

That comment brought it all out of her.

He was right, after all. She had accidentally scoffed at his chauvinistic proposition to supervise the teachers for a week and rate their performance.

And just like that, four geriatric men stared down at her as she thought of a million quips—comments, questions, and concerns she could have voiced all these years, most of them revolving around the board member's refusal to shave tufts of white hair horseshoeing liver spots on top of their shriveling heads.

Rhea had grown up with a brother, and in doing so, perfected the art of argumentation.

"Our school has one issue." She found her footing and steadied her breath. This was, at the very least, an opportunity to make a point. "We spend money in all the wrongs areas. The kids are smart, talented, and curious. Some of the brightest I've ever seen. But if you think sending one of your good ol' boys to watch over the school for a few days is going to increase test scores... then I could not disagree with you more. We need smartboards, laptops for the kids."

Another swell of bitter rage warmed Rhea's body. "You have no idea what teaching is like, and you expect to stop by and diagnose the problem just like that? Spend three years in that school, and you might begin to understand the shit we deal with. Otherwise, I don't want to hear a judgmental word leave your mouth. I mean, coming to the school and casting your opinions out on the rest of us, I'm sorry, but..."

Rhea needn't say more.

The crowd of teachers sitting around her shifted uncomfortably in their seats. They knew she was right, they all said as much in the safety of their inter-classroom discussions, but here they were too cowardly. She searched those anxious faces and found no ally. Only the cold surprise of someone doing what you always hoped but never had the bravery to do. And fear—she saw a lot of downright fear and the desire for this whole thing to end so people could return back to their miserably normal lives and never amount to anything, ever.

Who was she kidding? Her colleagues would never speak a word. Rhea was alone in her rebellion. Cast away from fellow educators because of her ability to critique a system founded upon the idea of healthy debate.

She glared at the familiar metal folding chairs everyone sat in so obediently.

Facing the board.

She'd been sitting in those same convenient chairs with grippy feet and sickly brown paint since elementary school. Rhea never left the world of academia. She never truly experienced the variety of a life well-lived. For Christ's sake, she'd primarily dated men in polos living off their father's fortunes, while growing their own fortune off pseudo-intellectual podcasts and hacky pyramid schemes marketed on YouTube. If she had to hear about another guy's natural genius at sales or the downfalls of Grant Cardone, if she had to be forcibly subjected to stroking another massive ego stemming from a severe Oedipus Complex, or if she had to undergo another terrible date to a party filled with coke-snorting doctors who thought they were supermen, she'd roofie her own drink to avoid the depression.

The whole idea of a loveless teacher over the age of thirty struck her as mediocre in comparison to the dreams she once had of being on stage, playing her own composition for millions, returning back home to a loving family.

This was her stage now, her role—a hysterical elementary school music teacher.

Her audience hung in the suspense of what she might say next.

She curled her hands into fists, fueled by a thirst for vengeance. "Don't you see how they're trying to strong-arm us?" She spoke to the crowd, every one of her fellow faculty's eyes wide with a clear yearning for whatever this was to end.

The second-hand embarrassment is too real for them.

A couple phone cameras pointed at her. Thankfully, she had the type of disposition that could take any amount of criticism given the right scenario. At this point, it seemed unreasonable to stop. She might as well try and get through to someone else and wake them from this matrixed illusion.

"They don't give us raises despite the rate of inflation, and expect us to work even harder on some Zoom *bullshit* after hours? All this talk about fixing things, but nothing ever gets done..."

If she could throw daggers with her eyes, every one of the board members would be dead.

"This is all a performance for them. Arguing with these five idiots is as hopeless as changing the educational system."

The silence in the room grew tenser than her violin strings.

This didn't even seem to be about the board anymore. A part of her wanted to see how far she could go before being escorted from the premises. It felt good to offload all her frustration—like biting into a cheesecake after trying to diet for a few days, or scrolling endlessly through her social media feed even though she knew that there was time to practice her routine. That sort of unconscious, primal satisfaction she'd been holding back for so long.

It felt so good to let go.

But she decided it better to leave before staging a meltdown worthy of viral infamy. Losing her education career was one thing, but being recognized as the crazy Karen woman everywhere she went was another. Besides, the board members and fellow teachers were unworthy of her ruined reputation—that would be too good of a show. A nearby teacher flinched as Rhea reached for her purse.

"Oh, grow up," Rhea said.

She had broken through a barricade the rest of the teachers were too scared to penetrate. Their glazed expressions looked ghostly as she walked through the rows of collapsible chairs, realizing whatever barrier she'd broken through acted as a cleansing. The world seemed brighter than before, and filled with possibility. She could literally do anything she wanted. How liberating was that?

They'll never change, she thought, walking out of the district office with the giddy urge to smile. *I'm better off being poor.*

She would never be a teacher again, that was for sure. That chance had been ruined the moment she denounced the board and their little boy's club.

An electric buzz of adrenaline still lingered in her body; inner heat fending off the biting winter breeze. She wondered whether her sanity was truly slipping. She felt an *expansion*, like she would when her hands drifted freely over the piano keys, linking chords and notes in perfect harmony to create a story that somehow made all the more sense when she played the recording back to herself at the end of her routine. She only ever felt that way when she let her mind run free and she entered a flow state, as if her playful approach and subconscious knowledge of music theory allowed her to access the very essence of the world—*the ether*—waiting there to be discovered by a wandering mind, filtered through her fingers, and made not quite perfect.

Human.

She felt like a painter who took one huge step back from her canvas, gaining a wider perspective, and for once, in an oddly satisfying way, her life made absolutely zero sense. It was time to start a new project, and that excited her. Even Julliard seemed out-of-frame, and somehow, not as grand as whatever she could imagine.

But yeah, right now, everything was incongruous and out of place. She played the chords of her life a few octaves too low, the rhythm too quick. Her life's portrait made no clear sense, consisting of half-painted landscapes in one area, and abstract objects with no meaning in another, though it all might have made sense at one point in the past.

If Rhea was no longer a teacher, what was she?

—

Rhea entered her house, greeted by her barking dog. Little Lucy the Pomeranian wore a characteristic pink bow tilted to the left ear from her head-shaking habit. Her yipes demanded attention. Lucy didn't mind sharing her happiness in the form of cuddles and licks.

Letting the puff of white fur lay on her chest as she lay sprawled across the floor, Rhea stared at the popcorn ceiling, petting the dog while her mind drifted into a storm of dreary clouds.

With her dead-end teaching job and any relevant bridges burned to the ground, Rhea found herself exhausted of all profitable skills. She could always offer violin lessons, but that wouldn't pay her bills, or anything else for that matter. Who wanted to learn how to play violin these days, especially from her?

In every sense of the word, her past self would see her current self and think: *failure.*

I've made my mistakes. Sure.

Who hasn't?

How much of this suffering was her fault? She wasn't the one who made the school system a convoluted mess, too big for one person to fix. She wasn't the one who made her anxious personality distrustful of this entire fucked-up world.

It had always seemed like she created the song to her own life, painted on her own canvas, wrote her own story, but at this point, someone else appeared to be the author. She couldn't just start a new painting because this was the painting she'd been stuck inside.

I'm going to be sick.

If she had a husband to support her through something like this, she might have been able to use her new perspective to shift paths in a healthy way. With the right amount of time, she might have been able to get into school. He would have sustained and provided for her while she studied something concrete and actually useful to the world.

But even her love life was non-existent. She had no husband and no money, zero savings once you took into account her credit card debt, and not even the slightest hint of a love interest besides the janitor complimenting the crease of her outfits during after-school hours.

Her future told of a sad woman living with her parents.

She lifted Lucy off her chest in an existential stupor. The musky scent of pine wafted past her nose, followed by sweet, floral hints characterized by her last lost love—an ex, currently married and apparently capable of winding down, given the right woman.

The thought to call *Llswole* came to mind.

I'm so fucking desperate.

She imagined that a perfect, tall, hunk of a husband awaited her in the kitchen. A man who cared for himself enough to put on decent cologne and hold a job and didn't call his mother to settle their arguments or his father for money to throw at her, but did precious, thoughtful things like buy her flowers and hold the door open even though they'd been together for however long. She wanted to be that corny old couple in a cafe so badly.

But that life seemed to belong to a different version of herself, where she was on the big stage, looking out to see his proud smile in nearly every concert. Then, maybe she would be worthy of consoling on the nights when she felt this shitty, and someone would actually care to stick around and let her lay against his chest and listen to his heartbeat. That other version of her would be worth sticking with through anything, no matter how bad it got, because she was actually enough for him.

All I really want is someone who appreciates the person I am. Someone I can trust with my feelings. Is that too much to ask? I'm starting to believe it is. I actually don't think that person exists.

Her nose grew warm and stuffy as she made her way to the kitchen.

Time to eat the lovely dinner my husband prepared, she told herself, reaching for the second bottle of wine leftover from last night. *This is what I smelled.* A desperate laugh overcame her. *My body knows the type of wine it wants.*

Her problems would come at her one-by-one, thought-by-thought. She was prepared to match them sip-for-sip.

Wine glass filled to the brim, hair in a stringy mess, Rhea sulked toward the corner closet of her apartment with Lucy. She kept her set of violins there. They hadn't been used since her Julliard audition. After grading homework or bad dates, she'd think about the violins and her dream of leaving the stress behind, promising herself she'd play again soon. But it never seemed to be the right moment. Whenever she did pick up the instrument, she noticed how much her skills had faded in such a short amount of time, and that only made her sadder.

I'm going over to play, my love, she thought, drifting across the floor in a tip-toe dance that would convince anyone of her lost sanity. *No need to worry about me.*

Would you like some pastries? he would ask her. *I have some in the oven.*

Rhea's free hand floated to her chest and she gasped in appreciation. *I would love pastries so much.*

In this fantasy, her husband cooked pastries.

Before she knew why, every part of her body froze in a tense cord. Wine slopped up over the edge of her glass, spilling onto the floor as she paused on her toes, mid-dance.

If it weren't for the strange play she'd been acting out in her head, spinning as if deeply in love, Rhea would have missed the figure sitting in shadows on her porch.

He posed with such careful elegance that he might have been a statue. His posture remained so perfectly still, Rhea doubted his existence. She doubted her own mind. Nothing moved under the wrinkled black cloak, though the hood stared forward. Everything about the situation felt like a potential kidnapping, or worse.

One of the board member's friends, sent to teach me a lesson?

It's not a thief, they would have more caution, she thought. *And they probably wouldn't be dressed in a cape.*

This is some lunatic.

His presence wasn't the only thing off about him. It wasn't what made her suddenly pause. Rhea saw a faint violet glow, and a steady hum had picked up, coming from nowhere and all around at once, so faint and ancestral that she had to be losing her mind. She shivered, and her arms prickled with goosebumps that crawled all the way up to her neck.

Maybe he hasn't heard me.

She took a step back, only to freeze at the stranger's casual change in posture. His head twisted partially, neck craning, and his hood fell aside to reveal a pointed gray ear.

I've lost myself.

That fake conversation pushed me over the edge.

The soothing light that surrounded him, and the deep hum she'd been hearing, it all contradicted every fiber of her being that screamed *run.* As he stood, taller than anybody she knew, his cloak waved in the winter breeze, gleaming with an innate silver glow like starlight.

Rhea forced herself to back away from the sliding glass door. She thought of the pink taser in her bedroom all the way upstairs. *Too far.* Her gaze drifted to the knife block next to the refrigerator, then quickly back to the porch.

The intruder remained still. Dark hair shimmered with the violet light that seemed to belong to his very essence, or whatever world he came from.

This is so fucked, Rhea thought to herself, considering whether it'd be smart to wield a knife in her current state.

The longest few moments of her life passed and she finally reached the knife block, expecting the being to dissipate in a sudden flash of dissolving light, or something to mark the end of the illusion. When nothing happened, and the being still refused to move, Rhea started to laugh at the whole situation. Her hand stopped shaking to the point where she could sip her wine. All this, and she hadn't let go of the wine.

The thing didn't move, let alone disappear. Even if she was hallucinating, what could she do? Walk away? Rhea didn't feel comfortable approaching it. She could call the police, but with her luck, it would disappear right as they walked through the door, and she would be left to explain the call with a knife in one hand and wine on her breath.

If she opened the porch, she might get attacked. It could be waiting for her to do just that. She should definitely be armed.

"I don't mean to instill fear," a voice said—reserved, like the lightest pluck on a string, emerging from the deepest recesses of her mind. "It was never my intention to frighten you." When he spoke, Rhea felt each word deep in her stomach. His voice had a coated warmth, to the point where the words didn't sound like English—more musical, easier to understand. She couldn't help but note how perfectly clear he sounded despite the sliding glass door remaining between them.

She settled upon one of the knives with a respectably large handle. "W-who sent you here? How did you find out where I live?"

"The council," he said. "My mentors. I know it isn't typically how our queen is summoned, but they sent me here as punishment. Things are changing in our kingdom, and I fear this season will be the last opportunity for us to make life better for all fae. You are the future queen the compass portal has chosen, and I must say, it couldn't have found anyone more suitable to the role of our Asenath. Every fae will aspire to sit on a throne, and look left to take in your beauty, reminding them that all is fair and all is possible because your being exists. But for this to happen, as I dream, we must leave quickly."

If she heard correctly, there were flickers of vexation in the low voice.

The council... punishment...

He was talking about the school board and their genius plan of supervision.

13

AT FIRST SIGHT

"I am summoning the most beautiful female in all of the realms."
Aramis played into the pride such an idea might hold, unsure of
how to comfort the scared human before him. Could he test her
to see if she had the qualities he'd imagined, or would he be wrong to
so much as question the future queen?

She gazed through the glass barrier dividing them. Her back never
turned and she maintained a wealth of space between them, but the
fact that she hadn't run away told him enough. This was a being of
courage. If her species truly rejected magick, then his presence
completely shattered her grasp on the world. But the Asenath wore a
look of concern, not terrible fear. Something more curious.

He remembered to move with intention, despite the nerves that
shook him. Why was he so nervous? Their only difference was the
belief in one another's existence, and now here he was undeniably, and
so was she. Now it was time to bring her to back to Shadow Hills.

To convince her of his kingdom's glory...

"I told you not to make the first move," Erlick said. His form had
evaporated into nothingness, leaving only the imp's grumbly whispers.
"Sit back down. She's too scared."

But Aramis could no longer play this waiting game. He was sure by the few words she spoke—pure kindness in the face of danger—made her a candidate for a potential queen. She was someone who would consider the character of a being, not their baseline traits and what crafts they could and could not pursue. She might even find a kernel of good in Aramis's backwards kingdom.

Aramis swiped at the front of his cloak, removing any dirt that may have lingered from his time spent in the dungeons of Losamara. How much other would the Asenath be willing to tolerate, if he wasn't presenting himself in a pleasing manner? He hardly wanted to approach the Asenath for fear of his stench.

Although, he lowered his hood with his head-high, shoulders back in confidence, and when he first gained sight of the future queen, it seemed as if the portal had chosen the only female he'd ever known with a natural aura that seemed to shine from her very being. Her beauty had a calming effect, like gentle ocean waves lapping their way up warm summer beaches. Her passion and fear, like a storm in the sea, seemed to intensify the intense heat of her gaze.

Pressing closer to the glass for a better look, her beauty expanded with never-ending complexity like a blossoming flower the more he stared. A thousand questions reeled through his head, but he found himself too hesitant to move for fear of ruining something that might save the realm and his very soul.

He also didn't want to break the illusion of curiosity she had for him by fawning over her like some inexperienced animal. Even so, she would eventually hear of his flaws from the council, and he couldn't have it any other way.

She was much shorter than he, perhaps reaching up to the center of his chest. Apart from her intimidating beauty, the way she studied him made him feel scrutinized. The Asenath seemed unimpressed and entirely skeptical. Every action she'd taken thus far—the small dagger in her hand, which he accredited to a need for protection and not a desire to kill—displayed her courage and empathy. She didn't lay down and cower in front of him, as Sinisar or other male mentors might have predicted from a female, and neither did she cast him away. He couldn't have admired or respected her more for that. It made him want to rid himself of all inadequacies and prevail in every craft the

Asenath found interesting—he would learn all of the crafts, if he must.

He wanted to please the Asenath more than he did. There was no need to listen to Erlick when he spoke. Rather, if he wanted to be this female's king and eventually throw the council from the seats they plan to stay in forever, he had to sway her with words from his own heart.

Her thin eyebrows furrowed over wide eyes the color of cherry oak. Dark hair fell in thin strands over either side of her nimble shoulders and she breathed heavily with the knife extended out before her. The bare mocha skin of her chest reflected the poor lighting, body rising up and down at the pace of her quickened breath.

She was the silhouette, he knew. From the portal. Everything seemed familiar about the Asenath in the most peculiar way. Never had he met a human being, but her anxious mannerisms seemed understandable, which was why he felt comfortable taking another step closer. Without certainty, he felt a part of her didn't want to leave, accredited to the greater magickal force that brought them together, summoning him to this time and place.

What did it mean that she hadn't yet run or called for help? Perhaps, she felt a similar pull toward his being? They seemed to give one another a chance at proving their good intentions, yet both were hesitant to seize the opportunity.

He took another cautious step forward, hands clasped at his waist.

"You plan to keep moving like a tree?" Erlick asked. "I didn't know I'd have to push you off the edge, given how eager you were back in the Hills. At least wipe that stupid look off your fac, will you? Please? Act like you've been here before. Like all of this has happened already, and you just have to take the right steps. You're not the first to ever fall in love, you know. This has been done so many times it's practically a craft. Come on... Where is that unnecessary fae confidence when you need it?"

Aramis swallowed and nodded. All he could do was stare dumbly at the Asenath's paralyzing nature.

"Alright... Let's try a different approach. Humans begin their mating ritual with a bow from the male, kissing the female's hand. Why don't you give that a shot?"

Kiss?! Aramis couldn't help but look for the imp to see if he was serious, viewing nothing but gray wall.

"Not me, look at her!"

The Asenath seemed to notice his shift in attention, waving the dagger left and right. He lost her trust in that small motion.

"Tell me what you want." Her voice was slightly muted by the door, but the streaming tears on her face said enough. "O-or... I'm calling the police."

—

Rhea wiped her falling tears with the back of a single hand, still holding the chef's knife with the other. The absurd humor of the situation gave way to utter amazement once the being lowered its hood, cuffs of his sleeves falling back to reveal gray skin and pointed ears—dark, braided hair in some forgotten Native American style. More than that, his concerned brows over cheekbones and words that cut to her very soul—it all displayed her own personalized psychosis.

Calling the cops would do nothing but lock her in an institution, but she had to threaten the hallucination somehow. Despite her threat, he moved with a sense of wonder and stability, looking like a character brought out of time from some Lord of the Rings fanfic.

Somehow, the genuine quality of his interest in her made the mental intruder seem as real as the faculty and board members. No... much more real. The fucking thing shimmered with beauty like some celestial alien. She'd expected a look of hunger from someone who entered her house unannounced and uninvited—a desire for rape or murder, she didn't know. Maybe both. But this wasn't a break-in at all. Rhea knew that this was different as soon as his hood lowered and he began to speak, seeing an entirely different person than the guys she'd met at bars. This thing sprung from her mind appeared to be more sympathetic than any of the councilmembers.

And she was actually thinking about giving in...

It had been forever since someone looked at her like this, as if she actually had something interesting and valuable about herself. His look made her feel important and wanted. This mental apparition also brought with it a state of wonder and possibility, if she only followed it. Fear of old myths and folktales always said not to follow the being, but they never really made it seem so perfect before, and they never made the character's situation as shitty as her own. Whatever this being was, it proved there was more to the world that rejected her. For once, Rhea was actually willing to hear out any part of the supernatural. The "natural" never worked out.

Moreover, the supernatural hardly seemed as dangerous as fairy-tales warned. If anything, the fae creature seemed frightened of her. She'd seen guys act like him in movies and books, but this creature looked like a tall athlete that had some sort of mild skin condition that made him the color of ash. He didn't even look different enough to be scary—in fact, the pointed ears and unsure way of talking added a rather cute sense of otherness. She actually understood the being in front of her. As far as she could tell, his nerves were genuine, and it made all of her skepticism come to melt away...

Unless he was with somebody.

And he claimed to be summoning a queen? From another realm?

What am I thinking... Can a hallucination even hurt me?

Could it possibly be good to play into the delusion? Could she come back to reality at the end of a conversation with a ghost, having some sort of improved outlook on the world and humanity, like Alice? Would she lose herself in Wonderland?

Her eyes were glued to the being who walked through her glass door. Why would she look away, even if she could? His ethereal, literally glowing beauty that brought along its own music only added to the insanity of it all. That steady, caring stare, as if desperate to learn who she was, melted through her.

She fought the urge to laugh, then she fought back a scream. Her control over herself wavered like a seesaw as she leaned—fell, bracing herself—against the kitchen island.

Screaming would do nothing but call for a trip to the asylum.

Maybe that's how I meet my future husband...

A policeman who first saw me pining over an imaginary creature with pointed ears.

Rhea still couldn't say she believed in it, whatever stood on the other side of the glass. Clearly, her mind entered a reality where her imagination became truth to her. As a result, it would make sense that the being would be everything she imagined from a partner and more. I wouldn't mind a pair of wings, she thought absently, surprised that enormous black wings didn't sprout from his back that instant.

If this was a result of a mental breakdown, she didn't understand why the being didn't disappear after she doubled down on his lack of authenticity and threatened to call the police. Wouldn't her own mind try and save itself? Even now, a gentle breeze of floral pine filled the air.

In the presence of his longing stare, it became difficult to speak. His lack of disappearance proved that he called her bluff.

"You said most beautiful in all of the realms?" she laughed, her abdomen sore from the switch between shock and humor. "Funny joke." She almost didn't recognize her voice. It sounded desperate.

—

The pounding of Aramis's heartbeat rivaled that of a war drum. He would do anything to ensure this female human returned to Shadow Hills. Becoming king and winning the tournament would be a different challenge, but after meeting the Asenath and losing his heart to her, it was a challenge he dared take.

Her voice also gave him fire and the bravery to answer.

He cleared his throat. "You say these negative things because you know the worst moments of yourself, and compare them to the best of others, and what others choose to show you. My queen... Do not be so harsh on your pure spirit. You know every wrong decision, every regret you've denied or admitted. Flaws way heavier on our conscious than accomplishments. But strangers, as I am to you now, only see what you are at this present moment. And my queen, what I see now is a woman beyond compare, brave and beautiful. Hurt, perhaps. Certainly thrown aside by a world that neglected her perfection. But I believe that it is only a matter of time before things get better, for us both."

He melted at the sight of the lowering knife, the tilt of her chin. The bottom of her eyes watered, and for the first time, he feared he misread the future queen. What was it I said? I will take it back a million times, to prove I meant no harm.

Erlick groaned next to him. "Would you stop with the soliloquies? This human is experiencing real fear. Ask for her hand to kiss, before she kisses you with that dagger."

"I'm not afraid of you," the Asenath said between breaths. "Y-you can't trick me. I don't know what you want, but this can't be anything good. It can't..."

"Why not?" Aramis asked, stepping forward until he remembered the Asenath wanted distance, and at that point, it didn't matter what Erlick knew about human mating traditions. "I would never allow anything bad to happen to you."

———

Where had she heard that line before? Um... Maybe from almost every fuck-boy she dated.

"Answer this," she said, smarter than to trust a strange creature's flattering words. Why did he sound like a knock-off, wanna-be Shakespeare? Was that really the best her subconscious could produce? "You came here to summon me because I'm the most beautiful girl in the realms..." She couldn't help but stifle a chuckle, probably looking psychotic with the knife in hand, mascara running from tears she failed to hold back. There's no way I can be beautiful to this thing right now... "That's ridiculous. You're ridiculous. How do you know, when haven't met every other woman, in every other realm?"

Thin gray slits shining at her like the moonlight, narrowed, and it made her wish she never asked the question.

"You're not real," she said. "Go away. Nothing you say or do can convince me otherwise. Please... Let me just spiral like every other person."

Silence worked its way into her bones and stomach. The way he towered in height scared her, yet his thoughtful demeanor teased his arm as a place for protection.

As if inspired, he said, "Just seeing you now illuminates my life. And I... I feel lucky to be here with you. I feel lucky to see how your beauty mimics the unity of the stars. I know you are our queen for these few reasons alone, though I could continue... We simply don't have the time, but if you do not come now, everything will not be as it should."

—

Erlick wouldn't stop whispering on Aramis's left, making it extremely difficult to focus. "Quickly," the imp said. "Obey their customs. Show your willingness to do, well... anything. That's what you promised, isn't it?"

Aramis had no issue dedicating himself to the new queen—he wanted to be the source of her happiness until the end of time.

With the glass still between them, he gave his best courtly bow. In addition to magick, this was not an act that male smith practiced.

"The knee," Erlick said. "Bend the knee."

Aramis couldn't help but glance up at the human. He must've looked ridiculous, but she had lowered the knife to the table.

My nerves have never been put to such a test.

"Forgive me," he said, knee still touching the ground. "I know my presence is beyond what one human might call strange, especially due to your lack of belief in my people. I know you don't trust my craft or my form. I..." He stopped himself. "I can only imagine what you must be thinking."

She laughed—not a good laugh. It was a cackling laugh of mistrust. "Thinking?... I'm not thinking. I've lost it, dude. I'm riding through limbo. Any ability to think has been long gone."

If she didn't want to come, he would leave her in Earthrealm—simple as that. It would be her decision with no questions asked. An Asenath who didn't want to be queen would only hurt the realm even more. And it didn't matter what punishments the council imagined—he would suffer through anything before subjecting the Asenath to a life she didn't want.

"Allow me to explain." Aramis cleared his throat.

"Good," Erlick said. "You take care of that, I'll speed things up." The imp suddenly re-appeared on the other side of the room, behind the Asenath. It took everything Aramis had not to watch the red form drifting through the air, hovering past an archway, into a narrow hall of doors.

"I don't think you can explain anything that I'll understand..." The Asenath spat without the slightest hint of distraction. "But are you real? I mean... actually real?" She repeated the last question through a fog of panic and confusion, looking everywhere in the room except at him.

"I am real. Perhaps a description of the state of my realm will convince you. You see, our council believes they know what's best for everyone." Aramis tried to speak with truth and dignity, revealing the heart of Shadow Hills without scaring its saving hope away. "We have a tournament, the Tournament of Hearts, and every year we summon a queen that is deemed suitable for our realm. This year, it was up to me to use the compass portal and find the type of queen our realm needed. I believed we needed a leader, someone unafraid to break barriers and old customs, to shout the truth while everyone else is lying..."

Her eyes had gone bleak. The queen gazed longingly at the space between them. "I hate the old ways."

"You know of our troubles?" Aramis asked.

"I think so. I can relate, at least."

To his right, the red form of Erlick flew back down the hallway of the Asenath's residence, through the arch. Aramis wanted to tell him to stop, to make it clear that he was so close to earning the queen's trust. She understood and wanted to hear more about the kingdom. If Aramis could explain the entire situation, he believed she'd willingly visit Shadow Hills, perhaps opting to stay. She didn't seem very happy in Earthrealm.

But shouting at Erlick would sever their growing, sensitive connection. Looking back, she already began to turn toward the arch.

He stood from his knee, but the movement alone frightened her. She dodged left, around the center table, her dagger brandished toward the arch.

—

"I'm sorry you've experienced such pain." The visiting creature continued to speak in his pleading voice. Throughout all this time, because of the shimmering cloak and the alien way he looked, it never occurred to her that he could've been lying.

Rhea jumped at the sound of skittering paws—Lucy sprinting across the wood floor. Her little pink bows rounded the corner, and at the sight of her owner, she erupted into a barking fit despite sprinting past her. Rhea could only watch, thinking the dog had been relatively late to come to her defense.

Lucy ran so hard toward the porch and sliding glass door without any sign of stopping. The fourteen-pound Pomeranian had seen the door open hundreds of times, but she still jumped at the glass, evaporating into thin air as soon as she struck the door. White fur, a pink bow, and a bushy tail disappeared all at once with nothing more than the sound of a fastened zipper.

Shortly after, Rhea thought she could hear that distant humming sound, a bit louder than before.

My dog didn't disappear... she told herself, but that was hard to believe when she saw everything with her own eyes.

"Lucy?"

She took a step forward, catching herself on the counter—her knife clinking against the marble. She snapped her gaze back to the elf-alien creature. Whatever the fuck he is.

Half-crying, she held the knife out in her tremoring hand. Her heart pounded too fast for her to breathe correctly.

"Where is my dog." Louder, when he refused to do anything but stutter: "WHERE THE FUCK IS MY DOG?!?"

The creature looked scared, panicking. His fingers roamed to his cheeks, pulling down the skin under his eyes. "I'm sorry. It's not what it seems. She is safe. That much I promise you."

"Don't promise me anything. Give me back my dog."

He looked to the side again; toward nothing. His gaze remained fixed on thin air. "How am I supposed to explain this?"

"Who are you talking to?" Rhea summoned her most threatening tone, which happened to sound much like the Pomeranian's bark.

Overlooking the being's much taller presence, she caught the nervous twitch in his eyes.

"Your animal is okay," he said. "She is in our realm."

"I saw her disappear." The words slipped out, numbed by whatever stupor Rhea entered. "She... disappeared. Just like that."

"The trip to my realm is seamless," he explained. "She will be there."

He spoke as if she had already agreed to go with him. "I don't even know you. You think I'll help you?" She wanted to forget a few moments ago, when she actually considered doing such a thing. It was the temptation of leaving this terrible world behind. She supposed that was what tempted most mental patients—the harsh reality of the real world. "I don't want anything to do with you. You're no different than..." The strangest word came to mind. Not kidnapper, but abductor. "Just give me my dog back and leave." She said while holding out the knife.

If my mental breakdown is powerful enough to make Lucy disappear, what might happen to me? For some reason, that didn't seem like the most important question to Rhea. The most important question was how this looked from the perspective of any outsider. What if Lucy was lying on the couch and hadn't barked once?

"I fear you misunderstand me," the being said.

"You want me to go with you to some distant place that doesn't actually exist."

"Shadow Hills is my home," he said. "A fantastic kingdom that could be yours."

"How do you know I'd like it there? You know nothing about me, but you say I'd be a great fit as your queen?" She'd seen Narnia and literally every other story warning of entering another world, the forbidden forest. But then there was the Matrix and Alice, who practically encouraged insanity.

"I did not choose you," he said. "It was our compass portal, a result of the most ancient magic we know. I am only the messenger and escort." A stoic sorrow permeated his frown. "I never meant to do that to your animal. I never should have."

My imagination knows very well how to pull on my heart strings.

Despite knowing the entire gimmick, those last words made her want to go with the fae more than ever. Here was a potential partner that actually apologized for their mistakes.

You're crazy, Rhea.

But why did she care if this beauty of a creature lived in the "real" world? What was that anyway, when she had such vivid dreams of playing the violin that didn't pan out? What was the comparison between the two promises she had to choose from? One world offered the potential to teach violin lessons or play for pennies on the street and lead a poor, miserable life, cut at the knees with every opportunity she gets, and the other world offered promises of royalty and fame— not quite royalties and fame, but enough.

Even if they were lies, Rhea had never been one to shy away from a dream, and she seemed to have exhausted all of her dreams except for this one option in front of her. This fake option.

You're giving in to the insanity. Escapism at its finest.

What did it matter to her? If she could return whenever she'd like—

The thought of disappearing with the creature shocked her for the first time with the wonder of adventure. What else waited for her on the other side of that "portal?" And if she left, who would be waiting here for her to return? Who would miss her? Not even Lucy, anymore.

She swallowed the nerves surrounding her next question. It helped to remind herself that this was an entirely fictional being.

"What would my responsibilities be as your queen?" She dismissed the unconscious desires that started to arise when those gray eyes regarded her thoughtfully.

"As our Asenath, you will rule over the kingdom for an entire season."

"Season?"

"Yes, roughly one-hundred years in human time. The amount of time it takes to train the upcoming class of competitors. Male fae will compete for your hand in a tournament of four games, and the winner will rule as your king."

"You won't be my king?" It didn't make sense that they would send him, and he wouldn't be her king. It made her doubt everything yet again.

He slightly shifted his footing. "That is for the tournament to decide, if you choose to bless us with your presence."

"I see," Rhea said. She set the knife on the counter and left it there for the first time since his arrival. "But can't you see why I'm hesitant? You're in my head. Something my mind created." Her mind said everything was wrong: an attractive being from a fairy tale shouldn't be in front of her like this. But that flutter of inspiration—the feeling that made her walk toward that violin, the throbbing in her chest that came along with dreams of performing on stage in front of millions, that feeling which she held so privately, and told to nobody in her life, for fear of it not coming true—it overcame her.

"I promise to do everything in my nature to be your king."

This was the adventure she needed, right? Everything she'd hoped would come along, just not in the way she expected.

"There would be no greater honor," he said.

"Yes, yes, okay," she said, speaking from that place of utter bewilderment, from which she created her best work and had her most fun. Not the safest, but the truest place, which always gave her the best experiences of her life. That seizing pain in her gut that could only be quenched when she made progress in what she wanted to do. "I'll go."

A question came to mind. She was so surprised she hadn't thought of it until now. It must not have felt comfortable before. "What is your name?"

"Aramis." He took another bow, his hand extended.

With shaking legs, she approached the glass door.

In her few remaining moments within Earthrealm, she wondered if it hurt to evaporate with such suddenness.

✢ 14 ✢

FEW AGAINST MANY

The compass portal and the pyramid containing it changed entirely from when Aramis teleported to Earthrealm. He found his footing in a dark cavern, hand slipping from the Asenath's—a force gently tugging her away, slipping with a *pop*. The hums and melodious chimes ceased entirely.

All of the tempting purple light the portal emitted seemed to evaporate, fading up around him, sparkling as he twisted and tried to find the future queen. The portal reeked like bittersweet tang, so strong he had to plug his nose to keep from sneezing.

It was too dark in the cavern to find her. That unsure, queasy feeling accompanying interdimensional travel felt easier to overcome the second time around, but the Asenath would surely want an explanation about what occurred, if she wasn't having trouble finding her own balance. Aramis didn't want her to worry.

"Are you there?" he asked the darkness.

Gasping breaths...

He navigated his way toward the rapid breathing to find the Asenath, crouched on the floor, her head tucked between her legs. Delicate shoulders bounced softly. When Aramis reached out to console her, he realized he hadn't gotten her name, only referring to her as his future queen. *So inconsiderate, I couldn't learn a thing about her before taking her against her will.* He couldn't help but curse himself, pulling away and switching his attention to the surrounding pyramid that once thrummed with summoning force but now looked ancient and abandoned. *I will be no use when it comes to protecting her if I can't even make her calm. If I'm not bright enough to ask for her name. Too nervous and unflinching.* His mind drifted to Brok, who likely would've made several moves, had the Asenath been before him. But then she would've been frightened. He would've come on too strong, and in a way, the potential for any real agency in the Asenath would be stripped away. Aramis wouldn't impose himself upon her, not even when she was in his realm, successfully summoned.

All violet glow receded, blending out into the darkness, allowing him to spot Erlick's red form floating near the ceiling. He had the initial urge to scream at the being for not giving him enough time to speak with the Asenath and allow her an honest decision, but perhaps the imp did what was best for the both of them—like he did now, flying high and out of reach.

Aramis realized he'd never again be able to find such an endlessly inspiring feeling such as what the portal gave him. Everything that happened from this point forth would be his downfall. Never again would he have the queen beside him...

A chill went through his body. He could never let that happen. Seeing the Asenath and bettering himself for her was everything he ever wanted in this realm. He'd finally found a woman who understood him. She gave him a chance, like he did her, and their fates were now intertwined in a way that would take most of him if they ever separated. And he was supposed to just let the council take her?

He couldn't help but feel guilty for the greed of his fellow fae.

Other than the Asenath, all sense of wonder and promise had left the pyramid, evaporating like water behind sodden gray stone and walls that reeked of dust. Silence heavier than the weight of his impending doom filled the space. *What will the council think about my success?* Erlick basically wrote off this part as smooth sailing, and Aramis agreed without question. He had some questions for the dim red shape flying toward him.

"W-What was that?" The Asenath asked first. "Where are we?" She climbed to her knees at the sight of Erlick, wiping her eyes, and she stood. It appeared her hesitancy to speak with odd-looking creatures fell away inside of the fae realm.

Her head twisted and lolled back, mouth agape as she took in the vastness of the pyramid's height, the massive bricks that seemed impossibly large, and then Aramis, her eyes wide and gleaming with mystery.

"*Another realm...*" The queen's gaze drifted to the side, along with her balance. She wobbled toward Aramis with a hand out in desperation.

He'd been quick to support her, trying his best not to savor the curve of her hips or the fruity scent of her hair as it drifted over him. "Breathe," he said. "This will all seem normal soon enough, but it will take time."

"Yeah... N-normal..." She leaned against him and clutched his forearm for stability.

Such proximity filled him with a racing energy, and yet, she leaned closer, sending waves of that paradisiacal feeling the pyramid had familiarized him with into the deepest, hopeless part of his soul.

"Everything will be okay. Are you healthy enough to continue forward? They await us below, but I am willing to sit until you feel better." He'd wait as long as she needed. The mentors could venture up here and drag them out for all he cared.

Her face flickered up at him in the darkness. Suddenly she pushed him, stumbling away, but he let her go only when he was sure she had balance. Fear permeated her gaze, gradually overtaking any curiosity that might have remained. She was hunched and shaking.

Erlick fluttered to their eye level, between them. Aramis had nearly forgotten about the imp. The shine of his red skin emitted enough light to see the queen's horror raising to utter disbelief. A tear streamed down her face. "You... What *are* you?"

"*Pff,*" Erlick scoffed. He shook his head, turning away from the Asenath. He slapped his hands against his satin loincloth. "Everything I've done for you two, and not a simple introduction." He harrumphed once more to state his point, then fluttered away. He flew through the narrow opening from which they entered, and into the main area of the pyramid. "Come," he shouted back at them. "It's not wise to keep unhappy fae waiting."

———

"I never thought it would actually work." Rhea practically lunged at the creature next to her before she could think better of it. Whatever happened to get her here, this being seemed the most eager to protect her. And the most capable.

Her heart raced with the possibility of how she could've ended up in this place created by her insane dream. Seconds ago she was pouring a glass of wine and looking forward to sulking in her broken dreams. "I never agreed to come here. I want Lucy. I can't... I... None of this is real."

Of course... that's it. I've passed through the barrier of reality, which can only mean one thing.

"Am I dead?"

———

Aramis didn't know what to say. He certainly didn't want to laugh. But *dead?* That seemed ridiculous in the realm of the fae, with life in every crevice above and below ground, with so much feeling inside of him.

But for a human, it might not seem so strange to imagine this realm as the afterlife, especially if the only thing he knew was a world without magick. He had to place himself in her shoes. A horned, dwarf-like creature flying through mid-air, feelings of intimacy with a creature she'd never met or known...

On second thought, all of this had to seem like the craziest Skooma dream to her, and it began looking that way even to him.

———

135

The penetrating darkness certainly felt like death, and the length of this Avatar-knock-off creature's reply seemed to provide her answer.

Rhea wouldn't write off the possibility that a handsome mystical being had been enough to alter her perception of the real world, prompting her to accidentally plunge a vegetable knife into her chest while she'd been under the impression of saving her dog. She could see the headline already: *Psychotic teacher has mental breakdown, killing herself with a Santoku knife.* Embarrassing, but she wouldn't be around to feel the shame. Maybe that was why it felt so good to surrender to his perfect little aura. Everything she ever had to deal with in the real world had no bearing.

Just admit that you're crazy.

You fell for a fantasy of soft lips and chiseled forearms.

Thankfully, when his eyes met hers, they seemed to hold a bit of understanding. "Before I answer, will you bless me with your name, my Asenath?"

That word sounded strange, though she remembered enough to know it resembled the meaning of queen. Either way, the subtle, unplaceable accent rolled off his tongue in a way that made her words stumble, as if each word were a pillar thrust up from the power of its deep, resonating tone.

"M-my name... Why would you want my name?" She spoke from a place of pure defense, trusting nothing here. She'd grown more hesitant after realizing that she wasn't simply hallucinating, but having a whole fucking trip. *What the hell was in that wine?*

"Names reveal the soul of a being," he said. "As does the method in which a name is revealed. For example, you are hesitant to reveal your name. You indicate mistrust."

"That's not true," she said. How dare he call her mistrustful when he'd dragged her to some unknown realm against her will? Who would ever in their right mind blame her for being hesitant?

A long silence endured, and in her periphery, she could see the glow of the red flying creature approaching.

"Rhea," she said. "If you have to know, my name is Rhea. Now can you answer my question?"

"This is not death," he said. "But another realm in space and time.

We exist alongside you, with parallels and differences, and the dark mages of our past spoke of the intermingling and co-dependence between realms." The creature stroked his defined jawline in thought. She found herself hoping that he thought she was attractive and meant it when he said he'd protect her, repeating it so many times. It was weird to admit that turned her on. Was that some sort of fucked up survival instinct?

"I like it," he said. "Your name speaks to a caring devotion toward your kin, along with those unlike you. The mother of gods and great mother goddess. It's no wonder the portal..." He trailed off. "What about me?" he asked. "Do you remember my name?" The question sounded so filled with hope that she'd almost forgotten through the sheer desire to remember. For the strangest reason—maybe it was how eager he asked—Rhea wanted to show her remembrance.

It came to her like the sudden rain of a storm. His name had a certain feeling attached to it, whether it resulted from the aura, her mind, this weird place, or the name itself... The syllables rose through her chest with a soothing warmth she hoped would never go away. To speak the name only felt right. "Aramis.... It's Aramis."

The darkness could have warped and wrapped around them for all the safety the name made her feel. Given the newfound comfort, she had enough inspiration for another question. "What is this place?" After realizing she'd asked that already, she changed direction, focusing on the being before her. "What are you, actually?" She glanced over ridges near his pecs and collarbone, curtained under long black hair that fell down a towering body, making her evermore curious.

He spoke with a calming clarity. "Simply put, to you, I am fae. A magickal creature from a place like your own, but different in many ways, the main being the way we embrace magick in this realm, and the magick that is embraced in yours."

She pointed toward the red glow, which poked its creepy horned head around the corner and watched them. "What is he?"

"My friend," Aramis said in an apologetic tone that sounded forced. "He prefers to get to know people by their first names before speaking. It is his custom, I suppose."

Amongst the beauty and grand nature of this place, Rhea found such pettiness hilarious. It was also funny how they expected her to be forward in a world they'd dragged her into. Was she to be treated like the *other* even in her imaginative after-life, or whatever this place was?

"Couldn't he have asked *my* name?" She asked the question loud enough for the red being to hear. "I can't read his mind to find out how he wants to be greeted." She caught herself before saying more. Pointing out people's flaws might not be the best idea in this place. The way the flying being studied her made it seem like she had dared to question some grandmaster.

"Keep that outlook," the fae creature said, garnering her attention once more. "It's the reason you're our next great queen." Aramis looked amongst the stone floor, seeming to choose his words carefully. "Would you care to come with us?" His open hand, extended to her, gave her a strange, exhilarating feeling of adventure, more than anything she'd felt on a date, but this was something close to love and attraction. Still, it was much stronger and slightly more anxiety-provoking. She never felt such a feeling before and didn't think it had a name.

"There is no need to fear," he said. "I will handle the introductions."

❦ 15 ❦
POLITICKS

Aramis figured the council must've devised a counter-plan, in case the tiniest sliver of possibility that he summoned the Asenath became truth. It irked him to try and guess what that plan could be. Already, he'd discovered most of the mentors were trying to keep him out of the tournament games. The divine mentor alone had attempted to fill his mind with an unknown potion. He wouldn't put it past them if, for instance, Lucilia used her irresistible golden light to seduce him and force that potion down his throat once and for all, escorting the Asenath away.

But would she be able to overwhelm Morian? The alchemy mentor would come to his defense, of that Aramis felt sure. Taking on Vis and Sinisar became an entirely different issue, to which Aramis had no solution. Those who wanted the tournament to continue were outnumbered. If it came to physical confrontations, Aramis would have no other choice but to fight, and likely lose.

He lowered his chin while exiting the pyramid, so close he could reach out and touch a stalagmite, glaring out of the top of his gaze as he guided the queen by her gentle, following hand, going wherever he went.

Aramis knew he might never get the chance to hold the Asenath's hand again. Because of this, he tried memorizing the lines on her palm, rubbing his fingers over the short length of her own and cupping it, squeezing gently despite wanting nothing more than time to explore the rest of the future queen.

Finally, he came to understand his punishment. After he gave the future queen to the mentors, he would only be able to stare at her from afar, amidst the chaotic trails of the tournament, if he were lucky. His nights would be lonely and cold and he would study the too brief inter-actions between them like perfect, intangible gems.

He wanted to warn the Asenath of her own trials that awaited, but feared panic would slip through his own voice, only increasing her nerves. It seemed the less he could elicit feelings of anxiety and stress, the better. He also wasn't sure what lay ahead for her, their fated paths soon splitting, and only wished that he could somehow have made their time in Earthrealm last forever.

Rather, Aramis said nothing as he guided her down the massive steps. The lack of ultraviolet glow and humming music felt eerily unceremonious, as did the mentors awaiting them at the last step. The pillars of illuminated flowers, more dilapidated than before, flickered and waned in crevices of rock, as if the rock were breathing, waiting to swallow them.

Yet, Aramis focused on the beautiful being of his responsibility, hoping with every fiber of his being she wouldn't resent him for having to part ways.

They developed a quiet routine, during which he lowered her stair-to-stair by her waist, wondering all the while what was on her mind. She didn't speak, and hardly moved despite small steps up to the next stair. When he picked her up she shook like a leaf with nerves. Over time, she'd come to expect his help, sitting on the ridge and waiting for his guiding arms. Her eyes drifted away more than once, taking in the magnitude of the cavern and the totems and the paths made out by a glowing fruit she had likely never seen.

As they neared the bottom of the stairs, Lucilia's bright glow, hardly dimmer than the flowers and the totems, pressed in at the corners of his vision. With each step, the Asenath grew more and more enamored by the divine mentor.

The four council members hushed one another like children caught sharing a secret, stealing glances toward the stairs. Nobody acknowledged them yet, which Aramis found strange. He took the free time to search for Erlick. If he hoped anyone to be here, it was the imp, though he spotted no subtle red glow in the midst.

Morian was the first to split from the group of mentors with no indication given to the others. His smile seemed sarcastic as he approached the bottom stair. Aramis reached for the Asenath's hand once more, struck with a wave of confidence when she quickly met his. Whatever the mentors had in store for him, he'd be happy to have this perfect gem, containing a perfect image of *Rhea*, the mother goddess.

Morian must've known human customs because he disregarded Aramis, taking the queen's hand and bowing, lightly kissing the skin below her knuckles.

She remained silent and firm as a board.

"You are a blessing to this realm," Morian said. "It seems as if our gifted fae has traveled to the ancient Gods to search for his queen. If the intensity of her intelligence is only half of her beauty, our kingdom will be safe."

The mentor's healthy excitement remained when he turned to Aramis, but his eyes oddly told of wide alertness. They studied him too closely, swept too carefully over his person. Aramis couldn't remember ever seeing the alchemy mentor smile this largely before.

"I assume your foray into the dark arts went well?" Morian asked, hands holding one another before him.

Aramis nodded; the answer was apparent in the Asenath's arrival. "It did," he added, loud enough for the other council members to hear.

The alchemist made no acknowledgment. He reached out and clasped Aramis's shoulders. He stared down at Aramis, as the three remaining mentors split from their circle, working their way toward the pyramid stairs and Morian's side. They focused on the Asenath, looking her up and down, as if pruning flaws piece by piece. Aramis couldn't make out what the alchemist tried to tell him, but as his arms lowered, Aramis knew something wasn't right. But when he scanned the other mentors and the cavern he saw nothing wrong or out of place.

Lucilia managed to make herself the most prominent of the four mentors, thanks to the golden light emanating from her skin. "My, my..." Her voice sounded like jingling bells. "She certainly is beautiful."

An unfamiliar sense of revolt inspired horrible thoughts of gouging out the mentor's eyes, kneeing Lucilia in the gut until she couldn't breathe, anything to keep her from taking one step closer.

Try to take her... Aramis thought. *Just try.*

How could Morian remain calm when he knew the council's intentions of remaining in power? Why was he smiling and doing nothing like an idiot? Why wasn't he questioning the fact that Vis and Sinisar crept toward him even as Lucilia approached the future queen, circling behind his resolute posture? Why didn't he turn to inspect them, backing away while wary of their sly movements, face shifting from a smile of acceptance to leering doubt and suspicion?

Aramis felt a patch of numbness spread up from the bottom of his feet, like standing on thousands of prickly needles, writing it off to nerves. Shaking his leg provided no help because he could not move it. The tingling sensation worked its way through his body, spreading up through his torso, like ice in his chest, out to his hands and fingers. It felt like being stabbed by an infinite amount of little swords slashing their way through his bloodstream.

He tried to turn and warn the Asenath, but he might as well have been sedated. Even if he could scream, nobody would hear him. Nobody would ever know that these mentors were trying to trick Aramis all along. Nobody but these four mentors would ever see that Aramis, an untrained male mage, successfully summoned the Asenath.

And what would happen to her?

We have to leave.

"Mentor," Aramis meant to step in front of Rhea, to pull her behind with a sweep of the arm and let her know that he was her shield.

His arm merely twitched. He couldn't move but a few inches, frozen in a half-turned gesture, facing the alchemy mentor who wore the same unbothered smile.

Morian wasn't blinking.

Rhea cried from his right, a frightened plea. He couldn't turn to see her. She likely couldn't move, either. With all his effort in finding and encouraging the Asenath, he could not save his queen. He brought her here to suffer right in front of his eyes.

My punishment...

Aramis wanted to scream, but his jaw and neck were locked. Threats left his throat in the form of pleading groans over a raised tongue. "*DDDddughhh. Agghhhh.*" He swallowed accumulated spit. His throat muscles still worked. He still had to breathe. The mentors didn't mean to kill him. They only wanted to crush his soul.

I promise that you will die, he thought, with more clarity than expected. *I promise to kill every one of you.*

His thoughts were nothing but weightless objections. They succeeded only as distractions from the terrible reality that he failed his future queen.

She trusted me with her life.

I should've been more secretive, sneaking out of the pyramid in a different direction. He thought all of this despite knowing there was nothing he could have done differently. Where would he have gone? Another room in the pyramid? The mentors would've eventually found them. He never should've left the Asenath's realm. He never would have, if he'd known it was going to be like this.

Lucilia clicked her tongue, her golden light gleaming in his periphery. "Our future queen is unerringly bright."

"Bright?" Vis said, her timid tone mistakeable for the hot wind, blowing with odd strength throughout the cave. "I would describe her as *wild.*"

"Do not let the human's youth fool you." Sinisar continued to pace his calculated circle around Morian. He wore a bitter look of resentment. "Aren't we forgetting the summoner, and his lack of qualifications?"

Sinisar raised a sword that mimicked the length of his arm. It was the curved sword he crafted earlier; the one he'd used to slice his mark on the totem, doing his part in opening the compass portal. The metallic blade even maintained its lavender glow.

Morian the Alchemist remained as undisturbed as the totem poles themselves. Aramis couldn't tell whether the mentors were holding their peer captive by a similar numbing means, or if Morian simply didn't want to stop the coup. His arms-crossed, conservative stance looked like a castle guard, making it seem like the alchemist had a secret only he knew.

He didn't react to the sword brandished by Sinisar, curved slightly in the perfect '*J*' shape. Aramis was close enough to read in the runic language, *Father of Warriors,* etched across the blade, a slight divot carved into the center.

Sinisar tilted the sword so the hook aligned with the center of Morian's throat. "What an encouragement you have been to our budding male mage. You, mentor, are a splendid source of inspiration and bravery."

"Now," Lucilia interrupted. "Do not make this more of a mess than need be."

Sinisar frowned. "You mean to tell me how to achieve my own justice? No... This is a time when neither you nor the king will influence me. This young male will watch what happens when tradition is broken, and one neglects the necessary powers of their calling. He will see how defenseless his precious idol truly is." Sinisar's beady eyes cut through Aramis. "Are you happy that you've succeeded, *hmm*? Are you proud of the skills you've learned to summon this queen and make her suffer like so? Now we must take matters into our own hands as mentors, and clean up your mistake. I cannot wait to see how this new queen and her female forces will affect the tournament. I suspect a retaliation on part of the male forces by magnitudes... Are you familiar with the blood and light prophecy?"

The tear riding a lonely path down Aramis's face answered for him. *I can't believe I didn't see this coming.*

Sinisar measured the blade against Morian's neck once again, a master sculptor at work. A trickle of blood made its way down the mentor's neck, the stream steadily increasing its flow as Sinisar buried the sword deeper.

Wordless groans from Aramis.

Another unsettling giggle. "Let's wipe that smile off of your face."

The alchemy mentor's caring eyes stared a few feet to the left of Aramis. He hated how Morian seemed so at peace with that smile.

The blade worked its way up to Morian's lips as red seeped into the alchemist's shirt.

"I always hated the art of transforming matter," Sinisar said. "As if you have some sort of claim on what belongs in this world. Your kind is not meant for mentorship, but the underground, where scum like yourself can mingle." Sinisar, half-laughing, bent the curve of the sword at a downward angle.

Elbows raised, he twisted the sword's tip down into the slightly wriggling ball of Morian's eye. The eye squished inward, bending under the sword's pressure, as if poking a bag of water. And then the tip of the sword sunk in. Yellow-green puss oozed down Morian's cheek, into the crevice of his lips.

Aramis's stomach gurgled. The muscles in his eyes, neck, and the rest of his head twitched. No matter how much he tried, he couldn't look away.

In one swift motion, Sinisar pulled his sword from the eye-socket. A *pop* from the suction of the eye resounded through the rest of the cave.

The torturous sound most notable to Aramis was the wet *clap* against the floor; the gross juxtaposition of an eye rolling on stone, looking here and there without aim.

Wings stretched out across Morian's back. The mentor himself didn't move, smiling despite the dark hole in his face. The slightest groan emerged from his cracked mouth. A mixture of puss and blood leaked well past his chin.

Sinisar stepped back, admiring the breadth of Morian's wings before laughing even harder. He raised the sword's tip to Morian's other eye, stopping at the sound of Lucilia's voice.

"End it... His light is growing difficult to detain."

An audible groan, this time from Sinisar. The armory mentor lowered his blade around Morian's neck, adjusting and twisting his wrists to the perfect angle. Throughout the kingdom, Sinisar had a reputation for precise craftmanship.

The same way someone might cut open a sack of potatoes, or swipe casually at a training dummy, so Sinisar dragged the blade along Morian's throat. At the end of his cut, most of the blood flicked off the blade's end, which had gained a deeper ethereal glow. Sinisar inspected this reddened light, thick as fog, stumbling into Aramis's periphery, high on murder.

Morian's smile left his face as every other muscle relaxed, and he fell onto the floor.

Vis broke the near silence, inhabited only by the wordless sobs of Aramis. "I imagine you've gotten your vengeance, mentor Sinisar. You as well, Lucilia. I seem to be the only one without relief in this scenario."

"I've fulfilled your desires as of late. Need you anything else?"

"Perhaps a break from holding this human. It requires more strength to hold water than light."

"Fine then. Bring her there. I want our contestant to see the result of all this... insubordination." Golden light to the left of Aramis brightened.

"Should we not bring her to the king?" Vis asked.

"In time. I've learned a thing or two from our male counterparts, my dear flower, and I would like to spread my knowledge to our friend." The green eyes of Lucilia pierced through Aramis the moment they appeared. Already, he felt that familiar aching burn in his head. "The males taught me sometimes things must be done without a shred of consultation."

Warmth overtook Aramis, cozier than before. He wanted to give in so badly. Letting Lucilia win seemed more like freedom than defeat. At least he'd be able to move and speak. The beautiful light simultaneously gave him a sense of panic and the potential for escape.

Vis appeared on his left, carrying the Asenath on her arm. The sight of his future queen granted him strength to remain present, despite his head feeling as if it might explode with regret and sorrow.

It wasn't clear what they'd done to her, but she'd been hurt. The mentors made impossible spells seem effortless and they could've turned her blood to ice for all he knew. The Asenath didn't register Aramis after meeting his gaze directly.

This is the work of the mentor. If I can remind her of anything from before, even her pet, she might be able to resist the light.

Aramis managed groans with no syllables—open-mouthed cries.

Lucilia's glow rose to an irresistibly bright shimmer, though she stood to the side, keeping the Asenath in his view. Suddenly, Rhea brightened with awareness, snapping out from her stupor. She looked as if finally breathing after being trapped underwater. She searched in a desperate panic, then settled into place, feeling the clothes on her body, actually pinching herself.

Then she looked at Aramis.

He could see her trust wither away with the fall of her shoulders.

Wordless groans, but the mentor's spell rendered his apology impossible.

Lucilia's piercing green eyes drew the room's attention. Her wings carried her into his line of sight. She showed no regard for Morian's body below her hovering feet.

"How interesting," she said. "My light was brighter than ever. Can you explain why she insisted on looking at you first?"

"So their souls *are* linked? He was successful?" Sinisar posed the question with a fair amount of disbelief.

Aramis groaned. He would've given anything to have one last word with the Asenath.

Lucilia nodded, as if understanding. "I'd like to hear what he has to say."

Warmth spread from his forehead to his lips, soon searing through his jaw to loosen the area. Aramis wanted to scratch the bottom half of his face and get rid of the tingling itch, but his hands remained locked.

"Rhea..." he said, eyes wide. He couldn't blink, but her responding sobs made him carry on. "I'm sorry."

It felt so unnatural to speak, so powerless. He wanted to bow to her, grab her hand, and kiss her a thousand times over. To carry her out of this place of nightmares, to where they would be safe.

"What's happening?" she asked through watering eyes. "Why did you trick me? Where... Where has my mind taken me?"

"Not your mind, little one," Lucilia said.

Aramis felt his jaw locking again—his mouth remaining closed, as if bound shut.

"He is the one who did this," said the divine mentor. "Look at his face, and know it well."

His groans did nothing to protest.

She's wrong. She is lying to you.

But the Asenath stared at him, her face shifting to a pale, nutty coloring.

"It will not matter once you give her the potion," Sinisar noted.

"I'm sure she appreciates hearing the truth. Don't you, my lovely?"

Rhea suddenly wore a bright smile on her face. It was as if she rid herself of all pain in the matter of seconds. "What is the truth?" She posed her question with enthusiasm.

Rays of an orange glow established a blinding void; a paralysis of pleasure. Lucilia's light shone bright enough to block out everything but the two forms in Aramis's line of vision, and they were nothing but black silhouettes posed against the light. He could see Lucilia and her teardrop wings descending toward Rhea. The light felt good, the same way that picking a scab felt good. All the pleasure existed within an overlying texture of addicting pain.

"I want it all to..." Rhea licked her lips, failing to close her mouth entirely. "To be gone."

"I can help you, my dear." She raised a cylindrical vial to Rhea's mouth.

The Asenath drank. Glee entered Rhea's being and she jolted up, tipping back the rest of the contents on her first sip.

"There," Lucilia said. "Give into it, my dear."

Nothing but white finally consumed Aramis's vision. Liquid that tasted like crunched leaves and stale, watery honey soon flooded his throat, and it tasted delightful. The harsh texture brought with it a pulsating warmth that spread from his chest to his outer limbs, each heartbeat making him feel further and further away from everything he had failed.

I failed her, was his last thought before giving into the golden-pale purity.

AUTHOR'S NOTE

When I first sat down to write Tournament of Hearts, I knew it was going to be a challenge for me. I've written fantasy and science-fiction from the start of my writing career, but I began writing romance because I needed money.

Believe it or not, there is an entire world out there on the internet where a lowly writer can make worse than minimum wage slaving away as a romance novelist. I did this for about four years, eventually growing to enjoy the work and realize the genre has so much to offer readers from all different backgrounds.

But I have never written fantasy and romance at the same time. I learned so much researching within the genre and writing this book. I hope the pages above spoke for the many hours that have been put into this work from many people. Without them, I would not be writing today. You know who you are. *Thank you*.

I'm just now beginning to understand this whole independent author business thing, and as the owner of a start-up business, I don't have too much money to work with. But I still want to provide quality content.

Therefore, the greater Tournament of Hearts narrative was split into three digestible volumes, releasing monthly. If you would like to be notified when the next volume releases, click here.

Thank you so much for reading. I hope you'll be back soon to read more about Aramis and Rhea in *Tournament of Hearts: The Mage*.

- Austin

Book Release Link: https://forms.gle/pqGoYCmoyL8FZ5Uu5

ALSO BY AUSTIN VALENZUELA

Unholy: A Gothic Fantasy (novella)

DRAGONSPEAK

Isaac's Blessing

FEATURED IN

Beneath the Twin Suns: An Anthology

WANT MORE?

For more information about my upcoming books and short story collections, follow me on any of my social media accounts listed below. You can also subscribe to my substack, where every Friday I publish a new short story. Subscribers also have access to the entire back catalog of stories, early updates on book releases, and more.

Thank you for reading,
    Austin

https://www.instagram.com/valenzuela.austin/
    http://www.tiktok.com/@valenzuela.au
    https://valenzuelashorts.substack.com/

Milton Keynes UK
Ingram Content Group UK Ltd.
UKHW040905181023
430840UK00004B/246

9 798223 880837